Through the Pages of Change

K.C. BARNES

Contents

Intro   1

1. Chapter One   4

2. Chapter Two   9

3. Chapter Three   12

4. Chapter Four   15

5. Chapter Five   19

6. Chapter Six   23

7. Chapter Seven   26

8. Chapter Eight   30

9. Chapter Nine   38

10. Chapter Ten   43

11. Chapter Eleven   50

12.	Chapter Twelve	56
13.	Chapter Thirteen	63
14.	Chapter Fourteen	69
15.	Chapter Fifteen	72
16.	Chapter Sixteen	78
17.	Chapter Seventeen	82
18.	Chapter Eighteen	86
19.	Chapter Nineteen	92
20.	Chapter Twenty	97
21.	Chapter Twenty-One	103
22.	Chapter Twenty-Two	109
23.	Chapter Twenty-Three	116
24.	Chapter Twenty-Four	121
25.	Chapter Twenty-Five	127
26.	Chapter Twenty-Six	134
27.	Chapter Twenty-Seven	141
28.	Chapter Twenty-Eight	147
29.	Chapter Twenty-Nine	154
30.	Chapter Thirty	161
31.	Chapter Thirty-One	168

32.	Chapter Thirty-Two	174
33.	Chapter Thirty-Three	181
34.	Chapter Thirty-Four	188
35.	Chapter Thirty-Five	194
36.	Chapter Thirty-Six	201
	Acknowledgements	208

Intro

I used to believe I had everything under control—my life, my marriage, my future. Now, each day feels like an endless marathon where I'm always running, never arriving. Between the chaos of managing the household and chasing after two young kids, I'm constantly on the move, burdened by the weight of responsibilities that never seem to lighten. My marriage, once a sanctuary of shared dreams and quiet moments, is slowly unraveling into a series of strained conversations and unmet expectations. Every little task—from the overflowing laundry basket to the hurried school runs—reminds me that I'm carrying a load that feels too heavy to bear alone.

The ache of exhaustion isn't just physical; it seeps into every part of my soul. I'm overwhelmed, and the relentless pace leaves little room for a pause, for a breath, for myself. It's in these moments of solitude, when the world feels particularly cruel in its demands, that I find a flicker of hope in the unexpected refuge of books.

Working at the bookstore has become my lifeline—a place where I can step away from the relentless demands of everyday life and lose myself among the shelves. Here, I'm not just a tired mother or a wife struggling to keep a crumbling marriage together; I'm someone with a passion for stories, for the magic of words that offers a temporary escape. Hosting the book club is where I come alive. In those evenings, surrounded by fellow bibliophiles, I feel free to share my thoughts, to laugh, and to rediscover a piece of the person I used to be before life's burdens took their toll.

Yet, even in these moments of reprieve, the reality of my life persists. The unyielding responsibilities at home, the growing distance in my relationship, and the relentless march of time remind me that I'm at a crossroads. I'm tired of playing every role perfectly, of being the rock for everyone else. In the quiet corners of my bookstore and the heartfelt discussions of our book club, I begin to see that perhaps, within the pages of these stories, lies the promise of a new beginning—a chance to rewrite my own story, to find balance, and maybe, just maybe, rediscover who I truly am.

Chapter One

Every day feels like a relentless loop—a cycle of exhaustion and small moments of reprieve that slip away almost as soon as they arrive.

I wake up just before my alarm, my mind already tangled in the day's endless to-dos. I force myself out of bed without waiting for the alarm to scream its warning. In those first few moments of the morning, I manage to brush my teeth and take a quick shower, all while my thoughts swirl in a quiet chaos. I know what's coming next: the frantic rush to get the kids ready, the inevitable small crises that mark each morning.

Four-year-old Sam is my first challenge. Still wrapped in the comfort of his blanket, he resists every attempt to be dressed. I crouch beside his bed, trying to coax him with soft words and gentle nudges, but his stubborn protests make every second count. Meanwhile, twelve-year-old Carter is already half-awake, his attention glued to the glow of his phone. I remind him—again and again—to grab his backpack, but he barely looks up, lost in the digital world that seems so much simpler than the real one waiting outside.

Once the boys are finally dressed and fed, the morning takes on a temporary calm as I drop Sam off at daycare and see Carter off to school. I return home for a brief moment of silence before the chaos resumes. I sit with a mug of coffee in hand, relishing the quiet. Those few minutes of solitude are a rare luxury—a pause before the day's next act of balancing responsibilities and expectations.

My destination is Willow's Pages, a little bookstore just ten minutes from home. The store is a world apart from the whirlwind of my morning. Named after the owner's late daughter, the shop exudes a bittersweet charm: cozy, intimate, and filled with the scent of aged paper mingling with freshly brewed coffee from the café corner. There are fifty-five thousand books lining the shelves—a number that might seem modest compared to the sprawling empires of literature in larger stores, but here each volume feels like a trusted friend waiting patiently for its turn to be discovered. I shoulder the bulk of the responsibility for keeping everything in order, a task that often feels monumental, especially on days when the weight of it all seems too much.

As a child, I'd lose myself in these books, escaping to worlds far beyond the confines of my small town. Now, as a mother of two and a wife drifting away from the person I once knew, books have taken on a deeper, more poignant role. They're no longer just a form of escape—they're a quiet reminder of the dreams and possibilities that I once believed were mine to pursue.

Working at Willow's Pages is both a blessing and a burden. The slower pace of the store is a welcome contrast to my chaotic home life, and yet the physical labor of shelving, organizing, and managing the myriad details never quite stops. My shift runs from nine to two, a window that grants me just enough time to collect Carter from school and tackle the rest of the day's demands. It's a schedule that keeps me tethered to a semblance of order amid the disarray.

But then there's Saturday morning—the one time that feels like a lifeline. I host a book club that gathers a small, eclectic group of regulars in a warm, inviting space. In that room, the world softens. People lounge in comfy clothes, sipping on their favorite drinks, their voices mingling in animated discussion about the stories that have touched them. I can bring the kids along; the store even has a little play area, so I don't have to scramble for help. It's during those couple of hours that I can almost remember who I was before the weight of expectations and routine began to define me.

Today is Thursday, and as I make my way through the day, I'm constantly counting down the hours until Saturday arrives. Those two hours of shared stories and quiet laughter are more than just a break—they're my sanctuary, a place where I can breathe and reclaim a piece of myself that seems to have been buried under daily responsibilities.

After my shift, the day's relentless routine continues with Carter waiting at school and the inevitable trip to the grocery store. Thursday and Sunday are our shopping days—a predictable rhythm that keeps our kitchen stocked, yet somehow, even in its familiarity, it serves as a reminder of the unyielding demands on my time. Carter watches carefully as I cross items off our list, and I can almost hear his silent critique if I ever forget something important.

This is my life now—a constant juggling act of duties, desires, and dwindling moments of peace. The routine is relentless, each day mirroring the one before, each moment a struggle to maintain control. And yet, amidst the chaos, the world of words remains a steady beacon. In the bookstore, in the laughter of a book club meeting, in the gentle murmur of shared stories, I find fragments of hope—a reminder that even when every day feels like an endless loop of exhaustion and stress, there are still small pockets of freedom, waiting for me to discover them again.

Chapter Two

After the bookstore's gentle hum and the comforting chaos of book club fades into the background, I transition back into the familiar rhythm of home. The afternoon carries its own set of challenges—a subtle shift from the refuge of stories to the unyielding demands of everyday life.

I make sure to pick up Sam from daycare, navigating the usual hustle without pause. The ride home is a blur of parking lots and silent thoughts, a reminder of the delicate balance between gratitude and the weight of responsibilities. I never forget the long, arduous journey we took to build our little family, a journey that fills me with both thankfulness and an unspoken ache.

Once home, the day's tempo shifts: Carter retreats into his own world upstairs while I settle into the role of evening caretaker. The kitchen becomes my stage as I orchestrate dinner, always mindful that William's return at six demands not just a hot meal, but a semblance of normalcy. Today, I opt for a quick, uncomplicated dinner—a pre-breaded chicken breast warmed just enough, paired with a fresh spinach salad. I let myself steal a few moments of quiet joy, watching Sam's carefree antics in the living room before the evening truly begins.

I pour a glass of wine nearly to the brim, a small indulgence that steadies me, even as I know it will soon draw William's disapproving remarks. His criticism has become as routine as the ticking clock on the wall—a constant reminder of the changes in him, the man who once shared my laughter and dreams, but now seems distant and hardened.

Though he's never crossed the line into physical abuse, his anger manifests in other ways: broken cabinets and shattered doors serve as silent witnesses to his volatility. His drinking fuels a cruelty that leaves scars not just on our home but on me—etched in bruises and unspoken traumas. I recall one night too many when a simple refusal was met with a violent disregard for my pain. The memory is as raw as it is unwelcome, a secret weight that shadows every return to our worn leather sofa, where he sits in silence, either fixated on his phone or lost in a glass of whiskey.

The slow, deliberate ticking of the clock mocks me as evening draws near, each second an echo of the dread that builds inside. Once, William had been the man who could make me laugh until my sides ached, who could turn a gloomy day into one filled with possibility. Now, the silence between us is a chasm, filled with unspoken words and unmet needs.

In these moments, as I juggle the remnants of my day—cooking, tidying, and bracing myself for the inevitable return to a home that no longer feels like a sanctuary—I cling to the fleeting hope that somewhere amid the chaos, I might rediscover the strength to reclaim my life. Each evening is a testament to survival, a quiet act of defiance against a routine that too often leaves me feeling unseen and unheard.

Chapter Three

Friday mornings always arrive with a twist of dread. The end of the work week should signal relief, a brief taste of freedom. Instead, here in my house, Friday's promise is tainted by anticipation of weekend conflicts—loud arguments, incessant yelling, and a relentless fixation on football that drowns out any chance for joy. Sometimes, I steal a quiet moment at the park with the kids, the solitude a brief respite before the storm. Other times, we end up back at the bookstore, where the world feels a little less heavy.

Today, I'm behind the historical fiction shelves, methodically stocking the latest arrivals, when Lilly bursts onto the scene. "Elle!" she exclaims, her voice a mixture of warmth and exasperation. In that instant, the familiar clatter of our daily grind fades into the background.

"Hello, Lilly. Did you enjoy your mini-vacation?" I ask, forcing a lightness into my tone.

Lilly practically glows—she's just returned from a sun-drenched, four-day getaway in Cancun with her husband, John. They live a life so different from mine, one filled with effortless indulgence and endless possibilities. Every time I see them together, it stings a little, a reminder of the happiness I've been missing. Lilly isn't shy about telling me that I deserve something better, that I shouldn't settle for the life I'm stuck in. And though her words can be harsh, they also carry a genuine care that I cling to in moments of weakness.

Our conversation drifts between casual banter and the unspoken weight of my personal struggles. I find myself venting about our therapy sessions—once hopeful discussions now reduced to recycled grievances. Every week, I brace myself for the same pattern: a brief surge of progress followed by a rapid descent back into old habits. I can't help but wonder if Will even remembers the promises he once made, if he cares enough to follow through beyond fleeting moments of effort.

Lilly's eyes narrow with concern. "Where'd you go, love? You lost me there for a second," she says softly.

I offer a wry smile, the corners of my lips twitching in a half-hearted attempt at levity. "It's been a long week. Days blend together when nothing changes—and I'm just glad I get to see you tomorrow."

Her concern deepens, and for a moment, I wish I could unravel all the tension I carry in one long, unburdened conversation. But work isn't the place for tears—at least, not with customers around. Instead, I laugh off her worry, promising to save our heart-to-hearts for a quieter time.

"Come over for lunch after book club tomorrow," she insists, "John would love to see the boys, too."

I nod, making a mental note to let Will know I'll be away for a few precious hours—a small, silent rebellion against the suffocating routine. In that fleeting promise of escape, I find a spark of hope. Tomorrow might be just another day in the endless cycle, but at least it will be shared with someone who believes I deserve a better life. And for now, that is enough to carry me through another Friday.

Chapter Four

Saturday arrives like a breath of possibility—a day I've been waiting for all week. The bookstore buzzes with quiet energy as our book club gathers in its usual corner, a warm haven away from the relentless pressures of home. Our meetings are typically filled with familiar faces, but today, something about a new arrival catches my eye.

He slips into the group with an effortless charm. Tall—around five foot nine—with dark brown hair framing striking blue eyes, he exudes a magnetic allure. He's everything one might imagine in a leading man, and as he exchanges easy laughter with Lilly, I can't help but feel an unexpected twinge of jealousy. It's absurd, really—I've never even spoken to him—but there's something in the way his smile lingers on Lilly's face that makes my heart yearn for a similar connection. In that moment, I imagine a life where his gaze could unlock some secret joy, as if together we could rewrite all the miseries of my own script.

It sounds like something out of a movie: a charming stranger enters, sparks fly with an enchanting woman, and life momentarily feels lighter. Yet I know my story all too well—the only cinematic moments I've experienced have been in bleak dramas where hope is smothered by relentless pain. And then, almost imperceptibly, he shifts his attention away from Lilly and fixes his gaze on me. My pulse quickens and the air seems to still around me as I lock eyes with him. Lilly, ever intuitive, smiles and gently rests her hand on his shoulder before they drift away together, leaving me with a swirl of questions and a curious spark of hope.

As the discussion begins, I find myself momentarily lost in his quiet, mesmerizing voice when he shares the title of his book—a light, effervescent rom-com promising love and happy endings. His tone is deep and mysterious, each word wrapping around me like a secret I desperately want to uncover. For a fleeting second, I let my guard down, allowing the allure of his presence to ignite a long-dormant desire for connection.

Reality returns as I notice everyone's expectant eyes, waiting for my turn to contribute. I force a smile, determined not to let self-doubt cloud the moment. I remind myself that I've never believed I'm unattractive—even if life has made me feel unworthy at times. I am me: five foot seven inches of deep brown hair cascading past my hips, a body shaped by motherhood and lived experiences that I wear like a badge of honor.

I steer the conversation forward, opening up the dialogue about the latest book that has captivated Betsy—a chilling tale of a kidnapped child that momentarily sends shivers down my spine. Yet even as the discussion deepens, my thoughts stray to memories of past heartaches and unresolved arguments, whispering reminders of the life I'm desperate to escape.

When the meeting draws to a close and the chairs are carefully stacked away, I search for him—longing for a goodbye, a word, a spark to sustain the fragile hope kindled during our brief encounter. He vanishes into the crowd without a word, leaving me with a mix of disappointment and longing. Later, Lilly fills in the gap: his name is Alex, a financial advisor who's recently found himself widowed, adrift with his own burdens despite his considerable wealth.

There's a bitter irony in his presence—a reminder that perhaps I'm not the only one carrying too much on my shoulders. And as I lock up the bookstore that night, the taste of possibility mingles with the familiar ache of reality, leaving me to wonder if this unexpected encounter could be the first step toward reclaiming the happiness I've long forgotten.

Chapter Five

Monday morning finds me behind the counter at Willow's Pages, my fingertips dancing over familiar spines as if trying to recall a story I once knew by heart. The soft murmur of customers and the comforting aroma of aged paper blended with a hint of fresh coffee create a refuge that momentarily shields me from the weight of my everyday reality.

In this quiet haven, my mind drifts to the lingering echoes of last night. William's absence of warmth had been palpable—a silent retreat into his own world while I sat alone, haunted by unspoken promises and the growing distance between us. The memory of his weary, almost apologetic tone as he announced our impending "talk" still hangs in the air, a reminder of the slow unraveling that neither of us seems able to mend.

But here, among the stacks of stories and whispered confidences of well-worn pages, I find a brief reprieve. A familiar voice breaks through my reverie. Marie, a regular with a small, curious toddler in tow, steps through the door. Her gentle smile and tired eyes offer a moment of genuine connection.

"Hi, Elle. I'm ready for a change—I've had enough cookbooks," she confides with a playful sigh, as if shedding the weight of routine with each word. I guide her toward the shelves of light-hearted reads, carefully selecting a few romantic comedies that promise laughter and escape. In those interactions, I discover a sliver of normalcy—a reminder that while I can help others find solace between pages, I'm still searching for the narrative that will restore mine.

As the day draws to a close, the store's comforting buzz gives way to an unsettling quiet. Stepping out into the crisp evening air, I notice the familiar silhouette of William's car. Home feels heavier tonight, the atmosphere charged with unspoken tension. Inside, the soft sounds of children and the distant hum of a TV barely mask the undercurrent of discontent.

I enter the kitchen and find William slumped over his phone, his posture echoing the fatigue that has seeped into every corner of our lives. Without thinking, I mention the email—an innocuous message that shattered the fragile illusion of our marital routine. The simple, business-like note from one of his coworkers has confirmed my deepest suspicions.

"William, I saw the email," I say softly, the words heavy with sorrow and acceptance. In that instant, his eyes meet mine—a flash of guilt quickly smothered by defensiveness. Before I can brace for a litany of excuses, I cut him off. "I know what I saw. I know what I feel. There's no more room for lies."

The silence that follows is vast, echoing the emptiness that has grown between us over the years. In that quiet, I confront the painful truth: the slow, almost invisible cracks of our disintegrating marriage have become an unbridgeable chasm. It's a chasm that I fear has always been there, widening with every missed connection and every unspoken word.

Tonight, as I stand in the dim light of our kitchen, I realize that my life has become a series of unsolvable puzzles—each piece a reminder of what once was and what may never be again. Yet even amid the bitter taste of loss, I cling to the hope that, just like the stories nestled on these shelves, my own narrative might yet find a way to turn a new page.

Chapter Six

The bell above the door jingles as a mother and her little one step inside, their arrival a brief burst of warmth in the midst of my subdued thoughts. A child's laughter cuts through the silence, and I watch as the boy—around Sam's age—becomes captivated by a colorful picture book on a nearby shelf. In that moment, my heart clenches with a mix of tenderness and longing. I think of Sam, my precious little boy whose joyful calls of "Momma!" play in my mind, a sound that promises solace even when everything else feels so fragmented.

The comforting hum of conversation and the familiar scent of old paper blend with a delicate undercurrent of melancholy that seems to shadow every corner of my day. Yet, amid this gentle turmoil, a presence disrupts my trance. The door swings open again, and with a gust of cold air steps William, his hands buried in the pockets of his coat. His face is drawn, his eyes tired, betraying a weariness that has become all too familiar. He offers a stiff, barely-there smile as he greets me.

"Hey," he manages, his voice rough as if each word is a struggle. "I thought I'd pick up something for the kids."

I pause, the conversation between us always feeling like navigating a maze of unspoken resentments and long-held grievances. With a low, measured tone, I reply, "You can take one of the picture books from the back shelf. They love those."

Without a word, he turns and moves toward the back, and I watch him leave, feeling a tightening in my chest—a silent question of what we're even doing anymore. I swallow hard, determined not to let the well of emotion spill over in this sanctuary of books and gentle chatter. Instead, I dive back into the rhythm of my work, sorting receipts and double-checking closing times, each task a small anchor keeping me tethered to the moment.

Then, a familiar burst of joy draws my gaze. There, peeking shyly from behind the shelves, is Sam. His face is alight with pure delight as he clutches a crumpled drawing—a whimsical depiction of our little family beneath a radiant sun. His exuberant "Momma!" fills the space, and in that instant, the weight of the day seems to lift.

I drop everything to scoop him up, his tiny fingers gripping me as if to hold on tight to the warmth we share. "Thank you, Sam," I murmur softly, pressing a kiss to his forehead. His innocent smile radiates hope, momentarily banishing the cold tension that has long seeped into the corners of our lives.

Just then, William reappears, his eyes lingering on the tender scene between us. I offer him no greeting, no invitation to bridge the growing distance—only a quiet acknowledgment of the moment, and a silent vow to preserve the pure joy that still remains in my son's laughter.

In that fleeting, fragile moment, as the disorder of life swirls just beyond the bookstore's walls, I realize that even when everything feels broken and uncertain, holding on to these small shards of happiness—like Sam's drawing and his bright, unwavering smile—might just be enough to see me through another day.

Chapter Seven

Silence has its own language—one that speaks louder than any words ever could. That quiet, heavy stillness fills our nights now, where once our shared bed was a haven of whispered secrets and soft laughter. Lying here next to William, I feel the chill of his absence even in his physical presence. His warmth remains, but it's as distant as a memory, fragile and fleeting, like trying to hold onto shards of glass.

I remember the nights when our bed was our refuge, the place we'd confide our dreams and fears, letting our hearts mend in the soft glow of the night. Now, it's become merely a place to rest, a familiar space that no longer offers the comfort it once did. I've tried to believe that this is just a rough patch—a byproduct of the chaos that two kids and endless responsibilities can bring. But every night, as I lie awake in the dark, I'm forced to confront the truth: this is who we've become.

Today, I find myself in the kitchen, mechanically wiping down counters while the day's residue of unspoken words and unmet needs presses down on me. Sam's cheerful engine of toy cars is the only bright note in the background, while Carter's absence is as palpable as the silence that now defines our evenings. I glance at the clock, waiting for the inevitable sound of footsteps and the creak of the front door.

The door opens, and William steps in, his posture as rigid as the air between us. He leans against the doorway, his eyes briefly meeting mine before darting away. "Hey," he offers in a flat tone that does little to bridge the gap. I muster a weak smile, asking, "How was your day?"

"It was fine. Same as usual," he replies, his voice void of any real warmth. The space between us swells with every unanswered question and every forced greeting. I find myself dodging the deeper conversations—the ones that gnaw at me about where we went wrong and whether we're simply two strangers sharing a life. Instead, I ask about Carter, the only safe topic, and he responds with a shrug that says everything without saying a word.

Tension clings to us like a second skin, each unspoken sentiment a reminder of the growing distance that neither of us has the strength to confront. I offer a tentative invitation for him to join me in putting Sam to bed, only to be met with a hesitant, "I'll be in later." It's as if that small departure is another door closing on the remnants of our togetherness.

The night wears on, and I find solace in the simple ritual of bedtime with Sam. His giggles and gentle grip as I tickle him bring a momentary reprieve from the weight of our fractured union. "I love you, Momma," he whispers, and for a fleeting second, I remember a time when love was enough to hold us together.

Returning downstairs, I find William alone on the couch, a half-empty glass of wine his only companion. I stand there, watching him in the dim light, the silence between us thick and unyielding. The echoes of our happier days—a time when we'd share dreams late into the night and the promise of tomorrow—seem to mock me from a distant past.

"You know," I begin softly, barely daring to break the quiet, "I miss us." My words hang in the air, raw and unadorned, as if they were a confession of a love slowly slipping away. He doesn't lift his gaze. "I know," he murmurs, his tone as flat as the night outside.

In that moment, the truth is undeniable: the love we once nurtured is now buried under the weight of our daily routines and unmet expectations. I wonder if missing what we had is enough to sustain us, or if we've already passed the point of no return. Yet, even in this solitude, the small, unyielding hope that the future might hold a new chapter lingers, fragile as a whispered prayer in the dark.

Chapter Eight

I hadn't expected to see him. I'd barely finished unlocking the bookstore, the soft chime of the doorbell still echoing through the quiet space, when I sensed someone behind me. I turned slowly and there he was—tall, with dark hair now interspersed with silver strands that spoke of time and experience. He wore a jacket that looked both worn and carefully chosen, as if he valued the beauty of things that only grew richer with age. His smile was gentle, but in his eyes I detected a trace of sorrow I couldn't quite place.

"I'm sorry to bother you," he said, his voice warm yet tentative—as if he wasn't sure he had the right to intrude. "I was at the book club meeting a couple of weeks ago. My name's Alex." For a moment, I froze. I'd seen him that morning at the meeting—a quiet presence who drifted in and out without fanfare yet left a lingering impression. His eyes had swept the room as though searching for something he wasn't quite sure he'd find.

"Alex," I repeated, my mind still catching up. "Right, of course. Lilly's friend?" It was almost unbelievable how easily I could recall those deep, thoughtful eyes.

He nodded, a small, knowing smile curving his lips. "Yeah. I've known Lilly for a while now. She's one of the few who kept in touch after... well, after everything."

A pang of sympathy hit me—there was more beneath his calm exterior than simple sadness. "I'm sorry," I murmured, uncertain of what else to say. "If you ever want to talk, I'm here."

Alex hesitated, his fingers idly tracing the edge of his coat as he gathered his thoughts. When he looked up again, his eyes shimmered with vulnerability and something like gratitude. He exhaled slowly, as if releasing a secret he'd held too long. "It's been hard," he admitted quietly. "I lost my wife a few months back—she passed unexpectedly. I thought that maybe... I don't know... that books might fill the emptiness, but sometimes I wonder if I've been reading the wrong stories."

The raw openness in his confession made my heart ache. I knew well the quiet void that follows such loss—the sensation of searching for something to make the pieces of life feel whole again. "I'm so sorry," I whispered, again, stepping a little closer in silent support. "That must be incredibly painful."

He offered a small, appreciative nod. "Thank you," he said, his tone steadier now. "I'm still trying to learn how to live with it. Lilly and John have been there for me—one of the few constants after everything changed."

I found myself grateful for Lilly's caring nature, a rare light in our often turbulent lives. "You're not bothering me at all," I quickly added, then caught myself, realizing how it might sound. "It's just... I didn't expect to see you here after the meeting."

Alex chuckled softly, a self-effacing sound that eased some of the tension. "I'm not exactly the life of the party," he said. "But Lilly mentioned you a few times, so I thought I'd drop in."

Curiosity bubbled within me. "Lilly mentioned me?" I asked, surprised yet intrigued.

"Yeah," he replied with a slight smile. "She said you work here and that you're kind. I didn't want to leave without picking up something interesting." I returned his smile, touched by his sincerity. "Well, can I help you find something?" I offered, gesturing toward the rows of books. He scanned the room, his gaze lingering on the shelves as if searching for an answer in their well-worn spines. "I'm not really sure what I'm looking for," he admitted softly. "Books... they're the one thing that never asks for anything. They're always there when you need them."

That sentiment struck a chord deep within me. Books had long been my refuge from the noise and chaos, a way to quiet the overwhelming weight of my thoughts. "Let me show you something," I said, leading him toward a cozy corner of the store. "We have a selection of classics over here, but if you need something to whisk you away, I'd recommend a good piece of fiction—something with a bit of adventure."

As we reached the shelf, Alex's eyes roamed over the titles before settling on a well-worn copy of The Catcher in the Rye. "You must have a lot of books," he mused. "It must be hard to pick just one. "I laughed softly and held up the book. "It's not about picking one," I explained. "It's about finding the one that speaks to you at that moment. Sometimes a book helps you forget, and other times it helps you understand."

Alex nodded slowly, carefully flipping through its pages as if testing its worth. "I think I've heard of this one," he said, his tone suggesting it might be exactly what he needed. "I'll give it a try." "It's a good one," I said, watching him with quiet interest. "It's about finding yourself amidst the messiness of life. Maybe that's what you need right now."

He offered a small, genuine smile—a rare moment of light in his otherwise pensive expression. After a pause filled with unspoken understanding, I couldn't help but ask, "So, how did Lilly describe me?" Alex raised an eyebrow playfully. "She said you were a bit distracted lately—something about your husband and all. She thought you might appreciate a quiet evening."

I let out a soft, surprised laugh. Lilly always had a way of saying what needed to be said, even if it stung a little. "I suppose that's true," I admitted, my voice softening as I met his eyes. "I've been preoccupied." For a long moment, we stood there in companionable silence, two souls acknowledging the weight of life's burdens without needing to articulate every thought. I wasn't sure where this conversation would lead, or if it was even supposed to lead anywhere. Yet in that space, I felt less alone—a shared understanding that sometimes, in the quiet corners of a bookstore, you find not just stories, but the solace of knowing someone else is struggling through their own.

For now, that shared understanding was enough.

***

The house is uncharacteristically still tonight. Carter is holed up in his room, headphones on, lost in a world of his own creation, while Sam sleeps soundly in the blankets I tucked him into earlier—his small, peaceful face a stark contrast to the turmoil swirling inside me. It's a peculiar kind of loneliness, one that creeps in not from solitude but from being surrounded by people who no longer truly see you.

I settle on the edge of the couch, the low hum of the refrigerator the only companion in this cavern of silence. William still hasn't returned; his absence is as familiar as the ticking clock on the wall, each minute stretching out as a reminder of the growing distance between us. Even when he is physically here, it feels as if we share the same space without truly inhabiting it together. I wonder whether it's worse to be invisible or to be a stranger in your own home.

A weight settles in my chest—a knot that refuses to loosen, no matter how many times I try to shrug off the pretense of normalcy. I've spent so long acting as if everything is okay, as if I can hold this family together, that I'm not sure how much longer I can keep up the act. Tonight, I let the silence wash over me, my fingers tracing the worn fabric of the couch—a fabric as familiar as the creases etched into my own skin. I've sat here too many times, waiting for a sign that something might change; a look, a word, anything to let me know that he still sees me.

My gaze drifts to the family photos on the wall—images of happier times, moments before we stopped trying to bridge the growing gap between us. Once, those pictures were a celebration of the dreams we had built together; now, they're painful reminders of what's slipping away, of a future that feels as distant as the laughter that once filled these rooms.

I can't recall the last time William looked at me—not with the warmth and wonder of when we first fell in love, when every glance spoke volumes and every touch reaffirmed that I was his whole world. Now, our conversations are reduced to logistics: who's handling Sam's preschool drop-offs, who's picking Carter up, who's making dinner. We've become two parallel lives sharing a space, roommates who no longer share dreams or even a genuine smile.

In the quiet of this night, as my thoughts spiral in the familiar cycle of longing and resignation, I face the raw truth: I'm tired of pretending that everything is fine. I'm tired of waiting for him to see me, to care, to remember the woman I once was. And yet, even in the midst of this solitude, a small part of me clings to hope—a hope that maybe, one day, we'll find our way back to each other. But for now, I sit in the silence, surrounded by echoes of the past, wondering if our paths can ever converge once more.

Chapter Nine

My heart pounded and my hands trembled as I stepped into the kitchen, where time seemed to slow down. I'd always been good at bantering with strangers over books, but facing William—the father of my children, the man I once dreamed of growing old with—felt like entering a battlefield. And yet, tonight, I knew confrontation was inevitable.

William sat at the kitchen table, absorbed in his phone, his thumb scrolling idly as if my presence were nothing more than background noise. I cleared my throat and said, "William," my voice firm despite the tremor I could barely hide.

He barely glanced up. "Mm-hmm?" he mumbled, lost in his own world. Taking a deep, steadying breath, I stepped closer. "I think it's time we talk."

At last, he looked up, his eyes flickering to mine before drifting back to his screen. "About what?" he asked, his tone cool and detached. "About us," I replied, my heart thundering in my ears as I inched closer, unable to escape the intensity of the moment.

For a moment, he merely regarded me with a mix of acknowledgement and indifference. "I thought we already talked about this," he said, his voice laced with a dispassionate weariness. "We've been through it all before, Elle. Things aren't great—but what do you expect me to do about it?"

I swallowed hard, my voice barely more than a whisper. "I don't expect anything from you anymore, William. I can't."

He set his phone down, and the air between us shifted—thick with unspoken truths. Meeting my gaze, he asked, "What are you saying?" I sank into the chair across from him, my hands clenched in my lap as the words, raw and unfiltered, tumbled out. "I'm saying I want a divorce. I can't keep living like this. We're not even trying anymore—we're just coexisting.

I never asked for a perfect marriage, but I can't keep pretending we're okay when we're not."

Silence stretched between us, more deafening than any argument could be. His lips twitched as if fighting back words, then he exhaled slowly, shoulders slumping in defeat. "I see," he muttered. "So this is it. You've made up your mind?"

I nodded, tears threatening to spill as I fought to keep them at bay. "Yes. I have."

William ran a hand through his hair, his eyes darting around the room as though searching for a lifeline, a remnant of the love we once shared. "I'm not surprised," he said, his voice eerily calm. "I know I've been distant. I hoped we could fix it, but maybe... maybe you're right. Maybe we can't."

His words stung with the cold weight of finality, each syllable cementing the truth I'd long dreaded. "Maybe this is for the best," he continued quietly. "I don't know what comes next, but maybe this is just how it's supposed to be." Inside, I wanted to scream—plead with him to fight for what we had, to try one more time—but I couldn't. Deep down, I knew it was already over.

I rose, each step away from him feeling like a farewell to the life we'd once imagined together. "I'm going to talk to a lawyer," I said, my voice cracking. "We'll figure out the details, but I can't live like this anymore." He said nothing more as I left the kitchen, the soft click of the door echoing like the final chapter of our shared story. Outside the confines of our fractured home, I pulled out my phone and dialed Lilly's number—the person who'd always seen through my forced smiles, the one who'd noticed every crack in the façade.

"Elle?" Lilly answered, her voice warm and laden with concern. "Is everything okay? You sound... different."

I exhaled shakily. "I did it, Lilly. I asked him for a divorce."

A pause stretched on the line as I listened to her processing my words. Finally, she spoke in a calm, steady tone. "Are you sure?"

"I'm sure," I replied, settling onto the edge of my bed, my hands still trembling. "I've been sure for a while. I can't keep pretending anymore—it's not healthy for me, or for the kids. I don't want them growing up in a house filled with silence and disappointment. They need to see that sometimes, walking away is the hardest but right thing to do."

There was a thoughtful silence before Lilly's voice returned, soft yet resolute. "You've been carrying this for so long, Elle. I'm proud of you. It's not easy, but it's the right choice—for you, for Carter, and for Sam. They need you whole." Her words broke through my defenses, and tears spilled over, unbidden and raw. "I'm scared, Lilly," I admitted, my voice barely above a whisper.

"I don't know what comes next. I don't know how to rebuild. I feel so lost... I don't even know where I'm going."

"You don't have to have all the answers right now," Lilly reassured me gently. "It's okay to be scared. But remember, you're not alone—I'm here for you every step of the way. You're stronger than you think."

In that moment, the crushing weight of my isolation began to lift, replaced by a fragile spark of hope. "I don't know how I'd do this without you," I confessed, wiping away my tears.

"You won't have to," Lilly replied. "I'm right here."

And as I sat there, listening to her steady voice, I dared to believe that maybe, just maybe, everything might eventually fall into place.

Chapter Ten

The sterile office felt more like a cold interrogation room than a place of support. I sat in one of the expensive leather chairs, the cool, smooth material a stark contrast to the heat of my racing pulse. My purse rested on my lap, and I found myself absentmindedly tracing the worn strap, as if seeking comfort in its familiar grooves. Around me, tall bookshelves stood like silent sentinels, packed tightly with legal tomes filled with dense cases, statutes, and precedents. None of it spoke to me of hope or reassurance—it only underscored the magnitude of the journey ahead.

I felt like a stranger here, playing the role of someone sure of her next steps when every fiber of me was filled with doubt. Across the polished table sat my attorney—a woman in her mid-forties with sharp glasses and an air of no-nonsense authority. Her hands were folded neatly in front of her, and as she began to speak, her calm, measured tone belied the weight of the words that were coming.

"First things first, Elle," she said, flipping through a thick stack of paperwork. "Divorce is a process. It's not something that happens overnight, and it's going to take time—possibly longer than you'd like. But we'll work through it, step by step."

Her words echoed in the silent room, and I nodded, feeling my throat tighten as I tried to focus on each syllable. She continued, her eyes locking onto mine with a seriousness that left no room for denial. "Now, regarding the family home—legally, one of you will have to move out. I know it isn't easy, especially with children involved, but one parent must take primary residence. The other will have visitation rights, and we'll work out a schedule tailored to your circumstances."

At her words, a knot tightened in my stomach. It wasn't merely the idea of moving that unsettled me—it was the stark reality that everything I had built in that home, every memory etched into its walls, might soon be uprooted. My pulse quickened at the thought of having to break this news to the kids, of watching their small world shatter into pieces.

"Custody will likely be split between both of you," she added, her tone clinical yet gentle. "Joint custody is common, but the details will depend on your arrangements. It's crucial that you and William communicate about this. And if there are any major disagreements, mediation will be necessary."

I nodded again, barely registering her words as they washed over me in a tide of anxiety. Joint custody made sense on paper—it was what was best for the children. Yet the idea of dividing my time with William, sharing the roles we once assumed as one, felt like a fresh wound. My voice came out quieter than I intended, "I understand."

Then her tone softened further, as if she were offering me a lifeline in this sea of uncertainty. "Elle, I know this is difficult. But you've already taken the hardest step by coming in today. You're doing what's best for you and your children. It might not feel like it now, but in the long run, this will lead to a healthier future."

I could only muster a small, trembling "Thank you," the words feeling insignificant against the enormity of what was to come. As she stood up to leave, promising to send the paperwork soon and inviting me to reach out if I needed anything else, I felt the weight of the conversation settle over me—a heavy, unyielding shroud. The road ahead was long and uncertain, but it was a road I knew I had to walk.

Leaving that cold, impersonal office, I stepped into the warm embrace of the bookstore. Instantly, the familiar scent of old paper mixed with freshly brewed coffee wrapped around me like a comforting blanket. For a brief, precious moment, the chaos and decisions of the day receded, and I allowed myself to breathe.

I was a few minutes late, my mind still tangled in thoughts of legal battles and shattered lives, but as I walked through the door behind the counter, the bookstore's comforting familiarity washed over me. Lisa, one of my ever-cheerful coworkers, greeted me with a bright, "Good morning!" Her smile, genuine and uncomplicated, lifted my spirits for a moment.

"Hey," I replied, returning her smile even if I wasn't sure I felt it deep down. "Is everything okay here?"

"Yeah, all quiet as usual," Lisa said, flipping through a list of new arrivals. "How are you?"

I paused, feeling the enormity of the changes I was beginning to face. How could I explain that while my life outside these walls was crumbling, here among the books, I felt a semblance of normalcy? "I'm okay," I finally managed, then quickly shifting gears. "Anything new in stock?"

Lisa's eyes lit up as she teased me, showing me a notebook full of titles and even inviting me to help arrange some new seasonal displays. In that moment, as we worked side by side, shelving books and discussing our favorite titles, I allowed myself to lose the heaviness of my thoughts. Each book I handled was like a small, tangible reminder that stories continued, that endings could lead to new beginnings—even if just on the pages of a well-loved novel.

Hours passed in this quiet, comforting routine until my phone buzzed in my pocket. I pulled it out, my heart skipping a beat as I saw Lilly's name on the screen. I answered, striving to keep my voice light. "Hey, you. What's up?"

Her voice, warm and full of care, cut through the haze. "I've been thinking about you, Elle. How are you holding up? How did the meeting with the lawyer go?"

I closed my eyes for a moment, steadying my breath as I arranged the new books on the shelf, the familiar texture under my fingertips grounding me. "It went... exactly as I expected," I admitted softly. "It's not going to be easy, Lilly. The lawyer said one of us will have to move out of the house, and we'll likely share custody of the kids. There's just so much to figure out—I'm not even sure where to begin."

Lilly's steady tone was like a balm. "Elle, I know it feels overwhelming right now. But you're doing the right thing—putting yourself and your children first. You don't have to have everything figured out today. Take it one step at a time."

I swallowed hard, trying to push down the lump in my throat. "I know. It's just so... heavy, you know? Everything feels heavy."

"I do know," Lilly replied, her voice imbued with sincere understanding. "And I'll be here with you every step of the way. You're not alone in this."

Her words, distant yet intimate over the phone, offered a small spark of solace amid the storm. "I don't know what I'd do without you," I confessed, my voice trembling as the weight of my vulnerability laid bare.

"You don't have to figure it all out alone," Lilly said gently. "And you'll get through this, Elle. One day at a time."

For a long moment, I stood there in the hushed sanctuary of the bookstore, breathing in the familiar scents and letting Lilly's words settle into my heart. In that quiet space, I began to realize that perhaps the hardest part wasn't sorting out legal details or dividing a life into fractions. Maybe the most challenging part was admitting that I deserved more—more hope, more wholeness, more of a future that wasn't defined solely by pain.

I took a deep breath, feeling a small but steady conviction rise within me. "I'll be okay," I finally whispered, the words carrying more truth than they had in a long time. "I will be."

And as I resumed my work, carefully arranging the stories on the shelves, I allowed myself to believe that, step by step, I might rebuild. In the quiet rhythm of the bookstore, with its soothing scents and gentle murmur of life, I found a promise—a fragile, yet undeniable promise—that tomorrow could be different.

Chapter Eleven

The day stretched on longer than usual. Time seemed to move at half speed, the hum of the bookstore filling the silence, but doing little to distract me from the weight pressing against my chest. I found myself stealing glances at the clock, watching the minutes creep by, counting down until I could escape this feeling—this restlessness that clung to me like a second skin.

The door chimed.

Instinctively, I glanced up, expecting another customer, another distraction to help pass the time. But when I saw who it was, my breath hitched. Alex. He stood just inside the entrance, hesitating for the briefest moment, as if debating whether or not he should be here. His dark hair was slightly disheveled, his sleeves rolled up just enough to reveal the strong lines of his forearms. There was something different about him today—an unfamiliar hesitation in the way he held himself, a slight unease in his posture. Then his eyes met mine, and something shifted between us, something unspoken but undeniably there.

And then, he smiled. That warm, easy smile that always seemed to scatter my thoughts, leaving me momentarily off balance.

"Hey, Elle," he said, his voice low, almost uncertain. "I didn't expect to see you here today." I straightened, forcing the sudden flutter in my stomach to settle. "Yeah, just another day at the bookstore," I replied, hoping my voice sounded steadier than I felt. "You know how it is." He took a few steps closer, slipping his hands into his pockets. There was something deliberate in the way he moved, like he was carrying something heavy—something he wasn't sure how to say.

"Actually, since you're here," he started, clearing his throat, "I was hoping to talk to you for a second." I frowned slightly, curiosity replacing some of my nerves. "Of course. What's up?"

He shifted his weight from one foot to the other, his gaze flickering away for a moment before locking onto mine again. I had never seen him like this—uncertain, almost vulnerable.

"Look, I know this might be... weird," he began, his voice quieter now. "But I wanted to ask if you'd like to... maybe grab coffee sometime?"

His words came out rushed, like he wasn't sure he wanted to say them at all, like if he hesitated even a second longer, he might lose the courage to speak them. "I mean," he continued, rubbing the back of his neck, "I know we don't know each other that well yet, but I've really enjoyed talking to you. And—" He stopped himself abruptly, exhaling sharply, frustration flashing across his face. "I'm sorry. I'm probably coming off all wrong."

For a moment, I just stared at him. I had never seen Alex unsure of himself before. He had always carried himself with quiet confidence, steady and sure. But right now, he looked like a man who had stepped outside of his comfort zone, unsure of where he was about to land. And then it hit me.

This was probably the first time he had done this since his wife passed.

The realization settled deep in my chest, a quiet ache forming there. This wasn't just about asking me out—it was about something bigger. It was about stepping forward, about letting go of the past just enough to see what might come next.

As if reading my thoughts, he hesitated before speaking again. "I'm not sure how to say this, but... this is the first time I've asked someone out since... since my wife passed." His voice was softer now, his expression raw in a way that made my throat tighten. "I didn't want to come across like I'm rushing anything. But I've been thinking about it, and... I'd really like to get to know you better. If that's okay."

His honesty caught me off guard, and for a moment, I could only stand there, absorbing his words.

He wasn't hiding behind charm or casual small talk. He was standing in front of me, vulnerable, asking—not just for a date, but for a chance to take a step forward.

I took a slow breath, letting the weight of the moment settle.

I thought about the conversations we had shared, the ease I felt whenever he was near. I thought about the way he listened, really listened, and how he never seemed to expect anything from me except honesty. Maybe it was too soon. Or maybe it wasn't about the timing at all.

I smile, and it feels like a weight is lifting off my chest. "I'd like that," I said, my voice soft but steady.

Relief flickered across Alex's face, and he let out a breath that sounded like he had been holding it for too long.

"Really?" His grin was boyish, unguarded, like he hadn't let himself believe I'd say yes.

I nodded. "Yeah. I've just started the divorce process, so... I think I'm ready to start looking forward to things again."

His gaze softened, something deep and understanding in his expression. "I get that," he said. "I've been there too, Elle. I know how hard it is to start fresh after everything falls apart. But I think you deserve to start over."

His words settled into my chest, unexpected in their depth. I swallowed past the sudden lump in my throat. "Thank you," I whispered, because I didn't know what else to say.

Alex took another step closer, his presence steady, grounding. "So... can I get your number?" His lips quirked into a small, playful smile, but there was something serious behind it, too. "I promise not to be too weird about it."

I laughed, shaking my head as I pulled out my phone. "No promises on my end." I handed it to him, and he typed in his number before passing it back. "I'll text you," he said, pocketing his phone. "And I promise—no pressure, no expectations. Just coffee."

"Just coffee," I agreed with a smile.

As Alex turned to leave, he glanced back one last time, offering me a smile that felt like the beginning of something new.

"I'll talk to you soon, Elle. Take care."

The door chimed softly as he walked out, and I stood there for a long moment, watching him go, feeling something shift inside me.

Maybe this wasn't just about moving forward.

Maybe it was about allowing myself to want something again.

I glanced down at my phone and saw the new message waiting for me.

Just making sure you have my number.

Looking forward to that coffee.

A small smile tugged at my lips as I typed out a response.

Me too. Talk soon.

And just like that, the weight in my chest felt a little lighter.

Maybe this was how it started—one small step toward something new.

Chapter Twelve

The days blur together. Between work at the bookstore, phone calls with the lawyer, and conversations with Lilly, I'm constantly moving but not going anywhere. Every night, after Carter and Sam are asleep, I find myself sitting alone in the dim light of the kitchen, staring at my phone, wondering what it all means and what this new beginning could look like.

But then, that morning, a message pops up.

> Hey, Elle. It's Alex. I hope I'm not catching you at a bad time, but I was wondering if you'd still be interested in grabbing that coffee this weekend?

I read the message twice, feeling a strange mix of excitement and hesitation. It's been years since I've allowed myself to be in a situation like this—where someone is genuinely interested in me. I'm not just trying to keep everything from falling apart. I'm not sure if I'm ready, but at the same time, something inside me stirs, urging me to say yes.

I take a deep breath and type back, my fingers hovering over the keyboard for a second before I hit send.

> I'd love to. How about Saturday afternoon?

A few seconds pass, and then another message pops up.

> Perfect. I'll pick you up at 2.

I smile at the screen, feeling a warmth spread through me. I don't know if it's the excitement of doing something just for me or the simple act of saying "yes" to something new. Still, I can feel my pulse quicken at the thought of seeing him again.

> Sounds good! See you then.

My heart is beating a little faster than usual.

I set my phone down, exhaling a breath I didn't know I was holding. This is it, isn't it? The first real step forward. The first thing that feels like mine is not weighed down by the heaviness of my marriage or the weight of all the "what-ifs" I've been carrying.

I decide to type out a quick message to Lilly.

> Alex is picking me up at 2 p.m. on Saturday for coffee!!

> I told you! He is so sweet and down to earth, you will have a great time. I am so happy for you!

> Thank you for all you have done. You really are a great best friend.

> Girl, I already know it. Have fun, but not to much fun. ;)

I laugh knowing exactly what she is hinting at.

***

Saturday comes quicker than I expected. I spend the morning tidying up the house, picking up toys and books—anything to distract myself from the nerves building in my chest. Carter and Sam are at my parents' house for the weekend, so the house feels quieter than usual. I find myself standing in front of my closet, staring at the clothes I've collected over the years. Everything feels too familiar, too tied to the past. I reach for a simple blue blouse, something comfortable but flattering, and pair it with my favorite pair of jeans.

I stand in front of the mirror, inspecting myself. For a brief moment, I feel a pang of doubt. What if this is a mistake? What if I'm rushing into things, dragging baggage from the past with me? But then, I look at my reflection again and realize—this is who I am now. The woman standing here is someone who has survived, someone who's ready to move forward, even if it's just one step at a time.

The doorbell rings at exactly 2:00, and my heart skips a beat. I take a deep breath and head to the door, smoothing my hands over my jeans as I go. When I open the door, there he is. Alex.

He's standing there with that same warm smile, his eyes crinkling at the corners as he looks me up and down. His hair is tousled, making him look more approachable and genuine.

"Hey," he says, his voice light but slightly nervous. "You look great."

"Thanks," I reply, my voice a little shaky as I step aside to let him in. "You're on time." He laughs, his smile widening. "I'm not one to make people wait. Not for something like this."

I feel my stomach flutter at the comment, and for a moment, I don't know if it's nerves or something else entirely. But I push it down because I need to focus on what's in front of me right now.

"Are you ready to go?" he asks, holding a car key in one hand and his other hand casually in his pocket.

I nod, feeling that old sense of anticipation flood through me. "Yeah, let's go."

The coffee shop is cozy, the kind of place where the air is filled with the rich scent of freshly ground beans and soft indie music humming in the background. We find a small table by the window, and Alex pulls out the chair for me before sitting down across from me. His posture is a little stiff, but his smile is warm.

"So," Alex begins, his hands wrapped around his cup, "I know we don't really know each other that well, but... I don't know. I feel like there's something here. Something worth getting to know."

His words are simple, but they catch me off guard. I wasn't expecting him to be so open, so direct about it. "I feel that, too," I admit, stirring my coffee absentmindedly. "But, I've got to be honest. I'm not exactly in the best place to jump into anything." Alex's expression softens, and he nods, looking down at his cup. "I get it. I really do. It's been a while for me, too, since my wife passed. I'm not looking to rush you into anything. I just wanted to ask if you'd be open to... seeing where things go, maybe?"

I can hear the vulnerability in his voice, the weight of his own loss still there, even though he's trying so hard to move forward. I understand that. In a way, I'm trying to do the same thing, even if I'm scared. "I'm just starting the divorce process," I say, my voice quieter now. "So... I'm not sure where I stand. But I know I need something different. Something that's just for me, you know?"

Alex's eyes meet mine, and there's a softness there, an understanding. "I get it. I'm not expecting anything right away. I just wanted to get to know you. I like spending time with you. And I'd like to see where that could go. If you're open to it."

There's a moment of silence between us, the weight of the words hanging in the air. But this time, it feels like a weight that can be lifted. Something that's not so heavy, not so complicated. Just... two people taking a chance.

"I'm open to that," I say finally, my heart beating a little faster. "I'm open to seeing where this could go."

Alex smiles, a look of relief spreading across his face. "I'm glad to hear that," he says, his voice light again. "We'll take it slow. No pressure."

As we talked, the conversation flowed easily, and I realized something I didn't expect. I'm allowing myself to take a step forward. I don't know where it will lead, but it's a step I need to take.

And this coffee is the first real thing that's been just for me.

Chapter Thirteen

It's funny how quickly time moves when you stop watching the clock. How a single day, stretched out before you with all its uncertainties, can seamlessly become a week. And then another. Before you know it, what once felt foreign and impossible starts to feel like the most natural thing in the world. I never imagined myself here. Sitting in a cozy little café, my fingers curled around a warm mug, the scent of cinnamon and fresh coffee drifting through the air, the hum of casual conversation filling the spaces between us. And yet, here I am—not just present, but at ease. I hadn't expected it to be easy, not after everything with William.

Not after years of strained silences, of walking on eggshells, of feeling unseen. But sitting across from Alex, I feel something I hadn't in years: the quiet comfort of being known.

There's no rush between us. No urgency. Just a slow, steady unfolding of something I can't quite name yet, but that I know I want to hold onto.

Our second date took place at a small Italian restaurant, tucked away down a quiet street. The kind of place that feels like a secret only a few lucky people know about. Candlelight flickers on the table between us, its golden glow casting long, soft shadows on the old brick walls. The air is filled with the scent of garlic and fresh basil, the occasional clink of glasses as people lean in closer, speaking in hushed tones as if trying not to break the spell of the evening.

Alex swirled the wine in his glass before taking a sip, his eyes never leaving mine. There's warmth in his gaze, a kind of openness I'm not used to but find myself drawn to.

"So," he says, setting his glass down and leaning back in his chair. "I've been thinking—I'd like to know more about your kids. I know you've mentioned them a few times, but I'm sure there's so much more to them than I know."

The question catches me off guard, not because it's unexpected, but because of the way he asked it—genuine curiosity, no underlying pressure. No one has asked about them like this before. Not in a way that makes me feel like their existence is an obligation, a burden. Instead, Alex asks because he wants to know them, not because he has to.

I smile, a real one. "Carter's twelve. He's smart, but also sarcastic—which, I have to admit, he gets from me." I laugh lightly. "But he's got this huge heart. He looks out for Sam, always making sure he's okay." I can feel my expression softening as I talk about them. "And Sam's four. A tornado of energy. He gets into everything. But he's also the sweetest little thing. His smile…" I pause, shaking my head with a quiet laugh. "It can melt anyone's heart."

Alex listens, nodding along, his smile never fading. There's something grounding about the way he pays attention, as if each word matters. "I'd love to meet them sometime," he says, his voice casual but sincere. "Whenever you're ready. I know it's a lot, especially with everything you're dealing with."

I expect to feel anxious at the thought, but I don't. Instead, there's a quiet understanding that I'm moving forward—not just for myself, but for them, too.

"I'll let you know," I say lightly. "Right now, I think we're still in the 'getting to know each other' phase."

He grins. "Fair enough. I'll be patient."

Later, as we finish dinner, the conversation shifts to lighter things. Music, movies. The kind of small talk that doesn't feel small at all. It's effortless. Comfortable. And it's only as I walk to my car that I realize something startling: I'm enjoying myself. More than I expected.

***

Our third date was different. An art gallery. Something I never would have done before. I wasn't sure if it was my scene, but when Alex suggested it, I found myself saying yes. The gallery is filled with abstract paintings—bold strokes of color, chaotic splashes of light and shadow. Some of it makes sense. Some of it doesn't. But all of it makes me feel something.

Alex stands beside me, his arm brushing against mine as we walk through the exhibit.

"You know," he says, his voice low, "I think some of this art feels like life. Messy. Unpredictable. But still... beautiful in its own way." I tilt my head, considering it. "I never thought about it like that. But you're right. It's like life just... happens."

He glances at me, thoughtful. "Sometimes I think the hardest part is just accepting that. Accepting that life doesn't always look the way you expect it to. But that doesn't mean it can't still be good."

His words settle into me, filling spaces I didn't realize were still empty. I've held onto so many expectations for so long. Expectations of what love was supposed to look like. What family was supposed to mean. But maybe he's right. Maybe life isn't about fitting everything into neat little boxes. Maybe it's about letting it be messy and finding the beauty in it anyway.

The divorce moves forward steadily. William hasn't contested anything. No fight over finances. No argument over custody. It's almost as if he's given up. And yet, I find myself waiting.

Waiting for him to do something. To fight. To care. But he doesn't. When I call Lilly, I voice my uncertainty. "It's eerie," I admit. "I thought it would be harder. I thought he'd put up more of a fight." Lilly is quiet before sighing. "Maybe he's just done. Maybe he knows it's over, too." I nod, even though she can't see me. "Yeah. Maybe."

But as I hang up, something inside me shifts. Maybe this is what letting go really looks like. Not an explosion. Not a battle. Just... silence. An understanding that what was, no longer is.

The next time Alex and I meet, we walk through a park as the sun sets over the lake. The air is crisp, carrying the first hints of autumn.

"You know," Alex says, as we sit on a bench overlooking the water, "I never realized how important moments like this are. Just... simple. Not too much. But enough."

I look at him, his gaze soft. "I get what you mean."

He smiles. "I think I'm really glad we're here. Together."

I nod, my chest tight with emotions I wasn't sure I could feel again. "Me too." And unlike before, I'm not afraid of what comes next.

Chapter Fourteen

I never thought I'd find solace in the company of someone new so soon. With Alex, it isn't grand gestures or sweeping declarations that pull me in—it's the quiet moments, the way our conversations stretch without effort, the ease of his presence beside me. And yet, a part of me still lingers at the threshold of something more, unsure of how much of myself I am ready to give away.

The evening air is cool, tinged with the crispness of autumn's slow descent. The park is nearly empty, save for the occasional jogger and the distant sound of a dog barking. The scent of damp earth and fallen leaves lingers in the air, a reminder of the changing seasons. We sit on the same worn bench near the pond, the water shimmering under the fading sunlight, casting ripples of gold and amber across the surface. A slight breeze stirs the branches above, sending a few leaves fluttering down around us like fragile confessions.

I glance at Alex, watching the way his fingers absently trace patterns on the rough wood between us. His expression is unreadable, lost somewhere between thought and memory. I hesitate, then ask, "What's been the hardest part for you? About starting over."

He exhales, his gaze still fixed on the water. "The silence," he says after a moment. "After my wife passed, I told myself I'd be okay. That I just needed time. But the truth is, it wasn't just the loneliness—it was the quiet. The kind that sinks into your bones. I tried filling it with work, with distractions. Nothing stuck."

I listen, the weight of his words settling into my chest. There's something about his honesty that unnerves me, not because I don't want to hear it, but because I understand it too well.

"I think I've been moving for so long, I forgot what it felt like to stop," I admit. "To just sit with myself, with my own thoughts. It's like I've spent years being someone's something—a wife, a mother, a caretaker. And now, I'm trying to remember who I was before all of it."

Alex turns to me then, his expression thoughtful, his gaze steady in the dimming light. "And who was she?"

The question lingers between us, and I realize I don't have an easy answer. "I don't know yet," I say finally. "But I think I'm starting to figure it out."

A slow smile tugs at the corner of his mouth. "Then maybe that's the point. Maybe we don't have to know everything right now."

I glance back at the water, watching the gentle ripples shift under the last light of the day. Somewhere in the distance, a child's laughter echoes—a fleeting, weightless sound against the growing night. The truth is, I don't have to have all the answers. I don't have to know what comes next. For now, it's enough to sit here, to let the quiet exist without fear.

Maybe, I don't have to fill the silence. Maybe I can just let it be.

Chapter Fifteen

The divorce is nearly final now.

The paperwork is signed, the financial split agreed upon. There are no more heated discussions, no drawn-out fights over custody or who gets what. It has all been resolved with an eerie kind of ease, as if we were business partners dissolving a company rather than two people untangling the life we built together. William hasn't fought me on anything—not the house, not the kids, not the terms my attorney proposed.

It feels... almost too easy.

And that unsettles me more than I expected.

A part of me had braced for a fight, for some kind of pushback. I thought there would be late-night calls, tearful arguments, maybe even a desperate last attempt to salvage something that had long since crumbled. But instead, there's only quiet compliance. Agreement after agreement signed without so much as a question.

It's hard to process.

There's no closure in his silence, no sense of finality in the lack of emotion. The man I married, the one I once built dreams with, has disappeared into the paperwork, reduced to a name on legal documents that will soon officially mark the end of what we were. I don't know if it's relief or disappointment that weighs heavier in my chest.

Some days, I go through the motions of my old life—sorting through emails, making school lunches, keeping up with the bookstore—while the reality of the divorce lingers in the background like white noise. Other days, I feel the shift more acutely, like an earthquake under my feet, unsteadying everything I thought I knew about myself.

But then there are moments that belong only to me. Moments where I am laughing over dinner with Alex, where the weight on my chest eases just enough for me to breathe deeply again. There is something there between us, something I didn't expect to find so soon—if ever. It's not just about filling the space that William left. It's not about needing someone to catch me before I fall.

It's about wanting to reach for something new. Something different. Something that, no matter how much I try to ignore it, is slowly growing into something real.

Still, I am caught between two worlds—the one where my marriage is fading into a memory and the one where Alex is beginning to occupy space in my life in a way that feels more permanent than I had prepared myself for. I am not ready for a full-blown relationship. Not yet. But I can't deny that I want to keep moving forward, to see where this could lead.

Then, the final divorce papers arrive.

I'm standing in the living room when I hear the knock at the door, and when I open it, the delivery driver hands me a thick envelope. It's heavier than I expected, more than just paper—it's an ending. I close the door, my fingers tightening around the package as I walk toward the kitchen. I set it on the counter and stare at it, my pulse hammering in my ears. This is it.

There is no going back now.

My phone buzzes, pulling me from my thoughts. It's Alex.

Are you free tonight?

I glance at the clock. It's almost seven, and for once, the house is still. The boys are at my mom's for the evening, and the quiet feels like an invitation. An opportunity to step away from the weight of everything, even if just for a few hours.

I am. Want to grab dinner?

His response comes almost immediately.

I'd love that. I'll pick you up in 30 minutes.

When he arrives, I notice it right away—something is different about him tonight. He's wearing a dark jacket, his hair slightly tousled as if he's been running his hands through it all day. His smile is warm, but there's a nervous energy about him, something unspoken lingering between us. It's not discomfort, not quite. It's... anticipation.

I tilt my head, studying him as I open the door. "What's going on?" I ask, the concern slipping into my voice before I can stop it.

Alex exhales, his fingers flexing at his sides. "I just..." He hesitates, running a hand through his hair again. "I wanted to ask you something. Something I've been thinking about for a while now." My heart skips a beat. I don't know what I was expecting tonight—a simple dinner, a night of easy conversation—but suddenly, the air between us feels charged, heavier with meaning.

I step aside, letting him in. "Okay," I say slowly. "Ask away."

He nods, as if steadying himself, and meets my gaze. His eyes are steady, but there's a vulnerability there that I haven't seen before. "Would you consider... being exclusive?" His voice is careful, as if he's trying not to push too hard. "I know it's soon, but I feel like we have something. And it's something worth exploring." He pauses, searching my face for a reaction. "I just wanted to know if you felt the same way."

The words hang between us, and suddenly, I am hyper-aware of my own heartbeat, of the way my fingers twitch at my sides.

Exclusivity. Commitment. It's terrifying. It's not that I don't care for him—I do. More than I ever intended to. More than I am sure I should. But I have spent so long untangling myself from the weight of my marriage that the idea of stepping into something new so soon feels like stepping off a ledge without knowing how far I will fall.

Still, the warmth that spreads through my chest at the thought of truly letting Alex in is undeniable. I swallow, forcing myself to be honest. "I do feel the same way," I admit. "But I'm still figuring out what this all means. I'm still healing, still moving forward from... everything."

His expression softens, and he nods, as if he expected this answer. "I get that," he says. "I'm not trying to rush you. I just wanted you to know where I stand."

I let out a slow breath, the tension in my shoulders easing. "I'm glad you told me," I say, meaning it. "I think we have something too. And maybe... maybe we can keep exploring it. But I need time. I think we both do." I hesitate, then add, "Just know that I'm not pursuing anyone else, even if I'm not ready to put a label on this yet."

A slow smile tugs at his lips. "I can live with that," he says, his voice warm. "I'm in no rush. I just wanted to ask." And just like that, something shifts between us. It's not a definitive answer. It's not a promise of forever. But it's something. A step forward.

Together. It's messy, and complicated, and uncertain. But I feel like I can breathe again.

Chapter Sixteen

Over the past few weeks, I've come to understand that moving forward doesn't mean forgetting—it means learning to carry the past differently. I've spent so long trying to hold everything together, afraid that if I let go of the weight of yesterday, I might lose myself entirely. But maybe shedding those layers isn't losing myself. Maybe it's finding who I was always meant to be.

Alex and I have fallen into a quiet rhythm—small, steady moments that feel effortless. An impromptu trip to the farmer's market, where we laughed over the odd shapes of heirloom tomatoes. Evenings spent walking through town, hands occasionally brushing, both of us pretending not to notice. A silent understanding settling between us like the changing of the seasons—subtle, inevitable.

Tonight, he's coming over. My boys are with William for the weekend, and the house feels almost too still without them. I linger in the kitchen, rearranging a vase on the counter, smoothing a crease in the tablecloth. The quiet is unnerving, the absence of scattered shoes by the door, the usual background noise of cartoons or off-key singing from the other room. I was so used to chaos that now, without it, I feel strangely untethered.

The doorbell rings, cutting through my thoughts. When I open it, Alex stands there, framed in the golden glow of the porch light. He holds a small bouquet of wildflowers—simple, unassuming, but somehow perfect. "Hi," he says, offering them to me, a hint of hesitation in his eyes. I take them, the delicate petals brushing my fingers. "They're beautiful."

"I saw them and thought of you," he says simply.

His words warm something in me, a quiet acknowledgment that I am seen. That I matter in a way that is separate from everything I have been to everyone else.

I step aside, letting him in, and we fall into an easy rhythm. He follows me into the kitchen, where I find a vase, and he leans against the counter, watching me as we talk about everything and nothing—how Carter made me laugh so hard the other day I almost dropped a plate, how Sam has decided he wants to be an astronaut this week. He listens intently, the way he always does, but there's something different about tonight. A shift in the air between us. A quiet awareness settling into the spaces we haven't yet filled.

As the evening unfolds, our conversation deepens. The usual lighthearted banter gives way to something heavier, something real. I set my glass down, looking at him, trying to find the right words for the question that's been lingering on my mind.

"How did you know?" I ask. "That you were ready to move on?"

Alex exhales, his fingers grazing the rim of his glass. "I don't know if I ever really knew," he admits. "For a long time, I felt like moving on meant betraying her. Like if I let myself be happy again, it meant I was leaving her behind." He pauses, his gaze meeting mine. "But then I realized that grief doesn't mean staying frozen in place. It means carrying the love forward, in a different way."

I swallow against the lump forming in my throat. "I think that's what scares me," I whisper. "That if I let myself move forward, I won't recognize myself on the other side."

"You will," he says, his voice steady. "Because you're not losing yourself. You're finding her again." The truth of his words settles deep within me.

"I think you're already doing it," he says, his voice low ."And I want to be here for it, whenever you're ready."

That's the moment when I realize it—this is it. The person I've been waiting for, not to fix me, but to walk with me while I fix myself.

Chapter Seventeen

The days pass quickly, each one blending into the next as I continue to navigate the changes in my life. William and I have settled into a routine with the divorce—custody arrangements, financial agreements, all the messy details. But there's something unsettling about how little he fights for anything. He never asks for more time with the kids and never protests about the house or anything else.

It's hard to reconcile the man I thought I knew with the one who's now so passive. I can't decide if it's a relief or a disappointment.

I'm sitting at the kitchen table, going over the final divorce papers again, when the phone rings. It's Lilly.

"Hey," she says cheerfully. "How are you holding up?"

I sigh, running a hand through my hair. "Honestly? It's a lot. The kids are adjusting, but I still feel like I'm carrying everything alone. And William—he's just... not fighting for anything. I thought there would be more of a fight. More emotion, even."

Lilly is quiet for a beat before responding. "I think this is a good thing for you. You have held on for so long in a marriage that wasn't going anywhere. You were the only one trying for years."

I let out the breath I was holding.

"I just want you to be happy, Elle. This is what you need. You have a man who worships the ground you walk on. He would do anything for you and those boys. It's time to move on from Will and let Alex love you how you deserve to be loved."

I don't know why that realization feels so heavy.

"You are right," I say, "I just can't believe this chapter of my life is over. It's for the best. We deserve more from life than we were giving each other."

"That's my best friend talking. John says hello, by the way."

After a few more minutes of talking, we hang up the phone, and I clean up the house before heading to get the boys.

***

Later that week, Alex and I met at the bookstore where I work. I'm stocking shelves, my mind drifting as I organize a stack of new releases. It's a quiet morning, and the usual hum of customers and workers fills the air.

"I brought coffee," Alex says, appearing beside me, a paper cup in each hand. He hands me one and takes a sip of his own.

"Thanks," I say, smiling up at him. "It's nice to have a little break from everything."

"I thought so," he replies, leaning against the shelf, his arms crossed casually. "You know, I've been thinking about something."

"Uh-oh," I laugh. "That sounds dangerous."

He smiles, the corners of his eyes crinkling in a way that makes my heart flutter. "Not dangerous, I promise. I've been thinking about how things have been going, how everything's been moving so quickly but also slowly. And I just wanted to say... I'm here. I want to be here if you'll have me."

His words settle between us, not heavy but full of possibility. I remember where I was just a few months ago—feeling lost, alone, uncertain of the future. And now, here I am, standing with someone who wants to be part of that future.

"I want that, too," I reply softly. "I just need time. It's all still so new, and I don't want to rush it."

"I'm not going anywhere," he says, his tone warm and reassuring.

I decide its time I believe the words he is saying and let him into my heart.

Chapter Eighteen

The divorce is final.

The words seem surreal, even though I've been bracing myself for this moment for months. Four months, to be exact. That's all it took—just a few signatures, a handful of documents passed between lawyers, and the quiet, unceremonious end to a marriage that once held so much promise. There was no fight, no last-minute plea to reconsider. William accepted every term without protest, signing his name to a life we had built together and then walked away.

It's done.

There are no more legal back-and-forths, no more difficult conversations about custody arrangements or who gets what. No more sleeping in the same house as someone who felt like a stranger. Just silence. An empty space where something once was.

For so long, I feared this moment. I wondered if I was making the biggest mistake of my life, if I was wrecking my family, if I was setting my children up for a lifetime of fractured holidays and forced conversations. I imagined regret settling in like a permanent ache, something I would carry with me always.

But now that it's over, all I feel is relief.

A weight I didn't even realize I was still carrying has lifted. There's no more waiting for the other shoe to drop, no more trying to convince myself that we could fix something irreparably broken. The unknown stretches ahead of me, and while that thought should terrify me, I find that it doesn't.

It's strange how endings can feel so much like beginnings.

That evening, I meet Alex for dinner at a new restaurant we'd talked about trying for weeks but had never found the time. The space is warm, cozy, the kind of place that doesn't try too hard to be impressive but somehow still is. Low lighting, the quiet hum of conversation, the scent of freshly baked bread lingering in the air.

He's already at the table when I arrive, standing to greet me with that familiar smile that always makes my breath catch. There's something about the way he looks at me—like he's seeing all of me, not just the pieces I choose to show.

As we settle in, the conversation flows easily, as it always does with him. We talk about our days, about the bookstore, about Sam's latest fascination with space and Carter's sarcastic but endearing attitude. But it isn't until the waiter clears our plates and refills our wine glasses that Alex leans forward slightly, his eyes searching mine.

"So," he says, his voice gentle but inquisitive. "What's next for you? Now that the divorce is final?"

I pause, swirling my wine in slow circles, watching the deep red liquid catch the candlelight. What's next? The question lingers in the air between us, heavier than I expected it to be.

"I don't know," I admit finally. "I think I'm still figuring that out. There's a lot to process. But I feel like I'm in a better place now. More... open. More ready to move forward."

Alex nods, his fingers tracing the rim of his glass. "That's good," he says. "I know it probably doesn't feel that way all the time, but you've come so far, Elle. And I don't just mean with the divorce. I mean with everything."

There's something in his voice that makes my chest tighten—not in fear, but in the kind of way that happens when someone sees you fully, when they recognize just how much you've fought to get where you are.

I set my glass down and reach for his hand, lacing my fingers through his. "I hope that wherever life takes me, you'll be there with me," I say, the words feeling both cheesy and completely true.

Alex's face softens, and I watch as something shifts in his expression—something tender, something hopeful. "I plan on it," he says, squeezing my hand.

After dinner, neither of us is ready to end the night just yet. The restaurant is near a small lake, and the air is cool but not cold, the kind of night that invites lingering. So we walk.

The gravel path crunches beneath our feet, and for a while, we say nothing, just existing in the quiet of the evening. It's peaceful, the moon reflecting off the water, a light breeze rustling the trees around us.

Eventually, Alex breaks the silence. "I don't talk about Mia much," he says, his voice quieter now, more thoughtful. I glance over at him, studying his profile in the dim light. He's staring ahead, his hands tucked into the pockets of his jacket, as if bracing himself. "She was in law enforcement," he continues. "Ten years on the force. She loved it—more than anything, I think. It gave her purpose. She was incredible at her job."

I don't say anything, just listening as he speaks.

"We talked about having kids one day," he says, a small, wistful smile flickering at the corner of his mouth. "But she wasn't ready. Her career came first. I understood that, even if I wanted more time with her. She had this way of making me better, of pushing me to be more. And then, just like that, she was gone."

His voice cracks slightly on the last word, and I stop walking, turning to face him. He hesitates for a moment before looking at me, his eyes glassy with unshed tears.

"She was thirty-five," he says. "They were supposed to be doing a simple raid. Intel said only the gang leader was inside. But the information was wrong. The whole group was there. A bullet caught her in the abdomen—just below her vest. They couldn't get to her in time."

A sharp ache grips my chest. I reach for him instinctively, wrapping my arms around him, holding him tightly. He lets out a shaky breath, his body trembling slightly against mine. We stand there like that, in the middle of the path, wrapped in silence and grief.

After a while, he pulls back, wiping at his face. "I don't think I'll ever stop missing her," he admits, his voice thick with emotion. "But I know she'd want me to move forward."

I nod, understanding in a way I hadn't before. Because grief is like that—it never really leaves, but it shifts, making space for something new.

"I can't imagine losing someone like that," I say honestly. "But I think you're right. She'd want you to find happiness again."

Alex takes a deep breath, nodding. "Yeah," he murmurs. "And I think I'm starting to." We continue walking, and though there's still sadness between us, there's something else too—something lighter.

As we near the parking lot, he reaches for my hand again, intertwining our fingers.

"Thank you," he says softly.

"For what?" I ask.

"For letting me talk about her," he says. "For understanding."

I squeeze his hand gently. "Always."

And in that moment, I realize something.

I'm ready to move forward.

With Alex.

Chapter Nineteen

The days after the divorce are a whirlwind of adjustments. The rhythm of our lives has changed, but we're slowly finding our way. Carter and Sam are navigating this new family structure in their own ways—Carter, with his teenage defiance and sharp wit, holds himself at a distance. He doesn't speak much about William, but I can see the questions in his eyes. I wonder if he's waiting for his father to show up in ways he never truly did before. Sam, on the other hand, is too young to grasp the depth of what's happening. His world is still full of superheroes and bedtime stories, but sometimes, in the quiet moments, he asks when William will come home. Those questions sting, but I answer them as gently as I can.

We're figuring it out together, and for now, that's enough.

Through it all, Alex has been my steady anchor. He doesn't try to fix anything or rush me into decisions I'm not ready for. He's just here, with patience and presence, making it clear that I don't have to do this alone. We've found a natural rhythm—one built on quiet moments, small gestures, and an understanding that doesn't need to be spoken aloud.

One thing I've noticed: he loves buying me flowers. They're never the same kind, always different, like he's determined to find the one I love the most. I told him once, early on, that I didn't have a favorite flower—that I didn't see the point in choosing when they were all beautiful in their own way. I only had to say it once. He listens that way, soaking up every detail as if the things I say are pieces of a story worth remembering.

Tonight, we're having dinner at my house. It's nothing extravagant—just something simple, something that feels like home. I want my boys to feel comfortable, to see that change doesn't have to be frightening. That new beginnings don't mean losing what came before. The kitchen is filled with the scent of roasted chicken and garlic, warmth spreading through the air as I stir a pot of mashed potatoes. The house hums with energy. Carter and Alex's laughter drifts in from the other room, an easy, natural sound that I hadn't realized I missed until now. I pause, listening to them, my heart swelling with an emotion I can't quite name. It's a quiet, comforting kind of happiness—the kind that settles deep into your bones, unshaken by uncertainty.

"Mom, can we have dessert after?" Sam's small voice cuts through my thoughts, and I turn to find him standing in the doorway, his eyes hopeful.

"You can have one cookie," I tell him, handing him a plate with a few of my homemade chocolate chip cookies. "But that's it—you need to save room for dinner."

"Yay!" he cheers before rushing back into the living room, the sound of his giggles carrying down the hall.

I smile to myself and turn back to the stove, stirring absentmindedly. A few months ago, everything felt fragile, like one wrong step would send it all crumbling down. But tonight, things feel different. Solid. Like maybe we're not just surviving anymore—maybe we're building something new.

Alex steps into the kitchen, leaning against the doorframe, watching me with that soft, knowing smile. "Everything smells amazing," he says.

"Thanks," I reply, brushing a stray strand of hair behind my ear. "I hope the kids like it."

He steps closer, wrapping his arms around me in a quick but deliberate hug. It's not grand or overly romantic—it's just reassuring, warm.

"They'll love it," he says softly. "They're lucky to have a mom like you."

His words settle in my chest, unexpected and deeply felt. I don't think anyone has said that to me since the divorce. I've spent so long trying to keep everything together, making sure my boys feel safe, that I never stopped to acknowledge my own strength. It's easy to believe you're standing still when you're moving so fast. But maybe, just maybe, I'm not just getting by anymore.

I swallow the lump in my throat, taking a breath before replying. "I think I'm starting to believe that."

Dinner is simple but perfect. Carter is unusually talkative tonight, recounting a prank his friend pulled in class, and Alex listens, engaged, laughing at all the right moments. Sam is content, happily eating his meal, clearly still thinking about the cookies he managed to snag earlier. There's a warmth here that I haven't felt in a long time, and I find myself soaking it in, memorizing every moment.

After dinner, we migrate to the living room for movie night—a tradition we started before things fell apart, one I was determined to keep. The lights are dim, the soft hum of the TV filling the space as the kids settle in. Alex sits beside me on the couch, close but not pressing, just there.

Sam curls up next to me, his head resting on my lap, his breathing slowing as sleep tugs at him. Carter leans forward, engrossed in the movie, and I glance at Alex, who is watching the screen but also, every so often, looking at me.

I realize that I feel whole. Not complete, not fixed, but whole in a way that makes me believe I'm moving forward instead of standing in the wreckage of what was.

I run my fingers through Sam's hair, letting myself be present in this moment. Because this—this is what matters. Not the past, not the what-ifs, but right now. The people who are here, the love that is growing, the life that is rebuilding itself in small, beautiful ways.

Alex glances over at me, and in his eyes, I see it—that quiet promise that we're in this together.

It's not perfect. It never will be. But it's ours, and that's enough.

Chapter Twenty

I never thought much about my health. Like most mothers, I put everyone else before myself—my kids, work, responsibilities as a wife, and later, as a single mother. There was always something more important, someone who needed me more. I was always the caretaker, the one making sure the house was in order, the boys were fed, the bills were paid, and my emotions were neatly tucked away where no one could see them. And because of that, I assumed I was fine. Life had already thrown so much my way—surely, it wouldn't dare add more.

But life has a way of surprising you when you least expect it. I didn't know that a simple doctor's appointment could turn everything upside down.

It started as nothing—a routine check-up, the kind I had put off for years. I hadn't been feeling bad, maybe just a little more tired than usual, but I chalked it up to the stress of everything—the divorce, adjusting to co-parenting, learning how to move forward. When I finally scheduled the appointment, it felt like an accomplishment, one small way to prove to myself that I was taking care of me, too. I thought I'd go in, get a clean bill of health, and be on my way.

I was wrong.

Dr. Reynolds had always been warm, familiar, the kind of doctor who never made me feel like just another patient. But when he called me back into his office after my blood work came in, there was something different about him—something in his eyes that made my stomach twist before he even spoke a word.

"So, Elle," he began, his voice softer than usual. "We need to talk about your test results."

The air in the room felt different—thicker, heavier. I swallowed hard, my fingers gripping the chair's armrests. The walls of the sterile office suddenly felt like they were closing in on me. The sharp scent of disinfectant made me lightheaded as I sat down across from him.

"Your blood work showed some abnormalities," he continued, pausing as if measuring his words carefully. "Specifically, markers that indicate a possible autoimmune disorder. It's not a diagnosis yet, but we need to do more tests."

Autoimmune disorder. The words felt foreign, distant, like they belonged to someone else. I blinked at him, trying to process what he was saying. My mind immediately jumped to the worst-case scenario. What did this mean? How bad could it be?

"Is it... serious?" My voice came out hoarse, barely above a whisper.

He sighed, folding his hands on his desk. "It could be. Some autoimmune diseases are manageable with medication and lifestyle changes, but others can be more complicated. We need to pinpoint exactly what we're dealing with before we know for sure."

My heart pounded. I thought about Carter and Sam, about the life I had been carefully rebuilding. Could I handle this? Could I be the mother they needed if my own body was betraying me?

"I—I didn't think anything was wrong," I admitted, my voice shaking. "I mean, I've been tired, but I just assumed..."

Dr. Reynolds nodded knowingly. "It's easy to dismiss symptoms when you're always taking care of others. But this is something we need to take seriously."

"Do you have any questions?" Dr. Reynolds asked, but his voice felt far away as if I were hearing it from underwater.

I opened my mouth but couldn't form any words. It was as if the air had been sucked out of the room. I barely heard the rest of his words. Something about follow-up tests, more appointments. I nodded numbly, agreeing to everything, but inside, I was spiraling. By the time I walked outside, the afternoon sun was blinding. It felt cruel, almost, how normal everything looked when my world suddenly felt unsteady. The drive home was a blur, my hands gripping the steering wheel so tightly my knuckles turned white. My mind raced—what would this mean for my kids? For my future? For Alex?

I parked in the driveway, staring at the front door. Carter was at William's for the weekend, but Sam was home. How was I supposed to process this with his small, innocent face looking up at me, asking for dinner, asking to be held? I had to hold it together. I had to be strong. The moment I stepped inside, Sam came running toward me, his arms outstretched. "Mommy, I missed you!"

His little voice, full of warmth and trust, nearly broke me. I bent down, scooping him into my arms, pressing my face into his hair, breathing him in.

"I missed you too, buddy," I whispered, squeezing him tight.

My smile felt like a mask. My heart ached as I held him close. The weight of what I had just learned pressed against my ribs, threatening to crush me. But for now, I had to push it aside. I couldn't let him see the fear in my eyes.

That night, after putting Sam to bed, I sat on the couch, phone in hand. My fingers hovered over Alex's number. I wanted to tell him. I wanted to hear his voice, to let him be the steady presence I knew he would be. But when I finally called, the words wouldn't come.

"Hey," he answered, his voice warm. "How are you?"

I forced a small laugh. "I'm okay. Just a long day."

"You sure?" He hesitated. "You sound... off."

I swallowed hard, gripping the phone. "I'm fine," I lied. "I just need some time to think. I'll be okay."

A long pause. Then, softly, "Elle, you know I worry about you, right?"

My chest tightened. He always knew when something was wrong, always knew when I was holding back. But I wasn't ready to say it out loud yet. Not when I still didn't understand what it meant.

"I know," I whispered. "I'll talk to you later, okay?"

"Okay," he said, but his voice was laced with concern. "Just... take care of yourself, Elle."

After we hung up, I sat in the dark, the silence pressing in around me. My hands trembled as I wrapped my arms around myself, trying to hold everything in, trying to keep from unraveling.

But the weight of it felt unbearable. Every breath felt too shallow. I wasn't sure if I was scared of the illness itself or of what it would do to my family. For the future, I have been carefully building.

It felt like the ground beneath me was cracking, and I had no idea how to hold it together.

Then, in the quiet, I allowed myself a moment of weakness. Just one.

I closed my eyes and whispered into the emptiness of the room, a plea, a prayer, a desperate hope.

"Please, let me be okay."

Chapter Twenty-One

The days after the doctor's appointment blur together. I try to keep up with my routine—wake up, get Sam dressed, get the boys out of the house, go to the bookstore—but everything feels heavier now. Every step, every action, every thought is weighted with the knowledge of what's looming. I feel like I'm moving through a thick fog, the world around me muted, distant.

I find myself noticing things I never used to. The way sunlight filters through the curtains in the morning, how the steam curls from my coffee cup, the sound of Sam's laughter echoing through the house. These small, beautiful moments should be comforting, but instead, they feel fragile—reminders of a life that might be slipping from my grasp.

I scheduled the follow-up tests with Dr. Reynolds, but I haven't been able to bring myself to look at the calendar on the fridge, where they are marked in bold, black ink. I know they're there. I know they're coming. But acknowledging them feels like giving them power, like confirming that something inside me is broken.

Alex has noticed the shift in me. He doesn't push, but I see the worry in his eyes, feel it in the way he holds my hand just a little longer, the way he lingers in our conversations as if waiting for me to let him in. But I can't—not yet. The weight of the diagnosis feels too big to share, too uncertain to speak aloud. What if saying it makes it real? What if I unravel, and he realizes I'm more than he signed up for?

So, instead, I pretend. I smile when I feel like screaming. I go through the motions, keeping the walls up, keeping him at a safe distance. But I know, deep down, that I can't keep it up forever.

***

The day of my follow-up appointment arrives too quickly. I sit in the small waiting room of Dr. Reynolds' office, my hands gripping a crumpled piece of paper with my appointment time scribbled on it. I've folded and unfolded it so many times that the edges are soft and worn, like an old dollar bill. My heart pounds as I wait, every second stretching out unbearably.

A text from Alex appears.

> Good morning beautiful, I hope your appointment goes well today.

Before I get a chance to respond the nurse calls my name, and I force myself to stand, my legs shaky as I follow her down the familiar hallway. The examination room is the same as before—sterile, cold, too bright. I sit on the crinkling paper-covered table, hands clenched together in my lap, staring at the clock as it ticks away the seconds.

Dr. Reynolds enters, his expression kind but serious. He sits across from me, folding his hands on the clipboard resting in his lap. I already know. Before he even speaks, I know.

"Elle," he says gently. "We have the results from your additional tests. We have a clearer picture now."

I brace myself, inhaling sharply. My pulse is erratic, my breath shallow. I've spent so much time fearing this moment, but now that it's here, I don't know if I'm ready.

"We've confirmed that you have lupus."

The word hangs in the air, unfamiliar yet suffocating. Lupus. It sounds foreign, like something that belongs to someone else. Not me.

Dr. Reynolds continues, his voice steady, professional. "Lupus is an autoimmune disorder. It means your immune system attacks healthy tissue, causing inflammation and damage to various parts of your body. It can affect your skin, joints, even organs like your kidneys and heart. But the good news is that, with the right treatment, it can be managed. You'll need medication, lifestyle adjustments, and regular monitoring, but many people live full, active lives with this condition."

My mind is spinning. The words aren't processing the way they should. Managed. Monitored. Medication. I want to grab hold of something solid, but I feel like I'm floating, untethered, disconnected from the body I thought I knew.

"Is it... serious?" My voice is barely above a whisper.

He nods. "It can be. Lupus affects everyone differently. Some cases are mild, others more aggressive. But you're catching it early, which is good. The key is consistency—with medication, with lifestyle choices, with listening to your body."

Listening to my body. The thought feels almost laughable. I've spent years ignoring it, pushing through exhaustion, stress, and pain because I didn't have the luxury of slowing down. And now, my body is forcing me to listen.

The rest of the appointment is a blur. Dr. Reynolds hands me brochures, schedules a follow-up, talks about treatment options. I nod, force a smile, promise I'll do everything he recommends. But inside, I feel hollow.

When I leave the office, the world outside seems too normal. The sky is too blue, the sun too warm, the people on the street too carefree. I sit in my car for what feels like hours, gripping the steering wheel, staring at nothing.

When I finally drive home, I move on autopilot. Park the car. Walk to the front door. Open it. The usual sounds of home greet me—Sam's giggles, the faint noise of the TV, Carter tapping on his phone. It's the same as it was before. But I am different now.

I close my eyes for a second, inhaling deeply before stepping inside.

"Hey, Sam," I say, my voice softer than usual. "Want to help me make dinner?"

He turns to me with a grin, his excitement so pure, so untouched by the weight of the world. "Yeah, Mommy!"

I kneel beside him, pulling him close, breathing him in. I don't know what the future holds. I don't know how much of my life will change because of this diagnosis. But in this moment, I know one thing:

I'm still here.

For him. For Carter. For myself.

And somehow, I'll figure out how to keep going.

After dinner I realize I never texted Alex back.

Hey Alex, I forgot to respond and the day just got a bit hectic after.

I hope you had a good day, I think I'm going to call it a night early. Goodnight.

I hope everything is okay. Goodnight beautiful. I can't wait to see you soon.

I smile then set my phone down on my night stand and fall asleep.

Chapter Twenty-Two

It's been a few weeks since my diagnosis, but the weight of it hasn't lessened. If anything, it's grown heavier, settling into the spaces between my thoughts, lingering in the quiet moments when no one is watching.

Every morning, for the briefest second, I forget. My body stretches, my mind groggy, caught between dreams and reality. And then it comes crashing down. Lupus. The word itself is small, but it carries an unbearable weight. It follows me like a shadow, whispering reminders of a future I haven't yet figured out how to face.

I look in the mirror and see the same reflection—same brown eyes, same hair that falls in soft waves over my shoulders—but I don't feel like the same person. There's something different now, something lurking beneath the surface. A fracture. A quiet, unspoken fear.

But I have to keep going.

That thought alone is what propels me out of bed, pushing me to start the coffee, to wake Sam up with a smile, to make Carter's lunch even when my body protests every movement. I have to keep going, even on the bad days—the ones where exhaustion clings to me like a second skin, where my joints feel like they're grinding against each other, where the very act of breathing feels like too much work.

I haven't told many people. The idea of saying it out loud, of making it real in the minds of those I love, terrifies me. I don't want pity. I don't want the tilted heads and soft voices, the careful phrasing of concern that only makes me feel more fragile. I don't want to be seen as weak. I fought to rebuild my life after the divorce, and now, just as I started to feel like I was standing on solid ground again, the earth beneath me has shifted once more.

But there's one person I can't keep it from.

Alex.

I didn't plan to tell him so soon. I wanted more time to process it myself before letting him in. But when he asked about my follow-up appointment, when he looked at me with that quiet, unwavering concern, I couldn't lie.

"You don't have to take this on alone," he had said after I finally admitted the truth. His voice had been steady, his hand warm against mine. "I'm here for you, Elle. Whatever you need."

His words hit something deep inside me, something I hadn't realized had been waiting to break free. I wanted to tell him I was fine. I wanted to say I could handle it. But the truth was, I didn't feel fine. I felt like I was unraveling, one loose thread at a time.

And so, slowly, I let him in.

We didn't have grand, dramatic moments—just small ones. A quiet dinner where he held my hand across the table. A walk in the park where he let me talk about nothing, about everything. The way he showed up at the bookstore with coffee just because he knew I was tired.

Alex didn't try to fix anything. He didn't offer empty reassurances or tell me not to worry. He just existed in my world, steady and certain, and that was enough.

Still, I was afraid.

What if this was too much? What if he realized that I wasn't the carefree woman he might have hoped for? That my body was working against me, that my future was unpredictable?

The thoughts consumed me until, one Saturday afternoon, I decided I couldn't hold them in anymore.

"Hey, want to grab coffee?" I asked him over the phone, my voice uncertain.

"Of course," he said without hesitation. "The usual place?"

"Yeah," I said, my lips curling into a small smile despite my nerves.

When I walked into the café, the familiar scent of roasted coffee and warm pastries wrapped around me like a hug. Alex was already there, sitting by the window, scanning the crowd. When his eyes landed on me, he stood, smiling in that way that made my heart stutter.

I sat down across from him, wrapping my hands around the warmth of my coffee cup, as if it could anchor me.

"I've been thinking a lot," I started, my voice quieter than I intended. "About the lupus. About... everything."

Alex nodded, leaning in slightly. "I'm listening."

I hesitated, the words tangled in my throat. "I'm scared," I admitted finally. "Scared that this is too much. For me. For us."

"You don't have to carry this alone," he said, his voice so sure, so steady, that it made my chest tighten. "I'm here. And I'm not going anywhere. You don't have to be strong all the time, Elle. You don't have to do this by yourself."

His words sank into me, settling in the hollow spaces of my heart. "I know," I whispered, looking down at my hands. "I guess I'm still learning how to let someone else be there for me."

Alex reached across the table, taking my hand in his. His touch was gentle, warm. "It's okay to need someone," he said. "You aren't going to scare me off because of a medical diagnosis. I told you I wanted to be in your life, and I meant it."

I blinked back the tears that burned at the edges of my vision. I hadn't realized how badly I needed to hear that.

The words felt like a balm, soothing a wound I hadn't even realized I'd been carrying. I realized that I was able to allow myself to believe that maybe, just maybe, I wasn't broken beyond repair.

I didn't want him to lose me like he lost Mia. I don't want him to feel the pain he feels when he thinks of her.

That night, as I tucked Sam into bed, I watched him sleep for longer than usual. His small body curled into his blankets, his chest rising and falling in the dim glow of the nightlight. Carter was at his dad's for the weekend, and the house felt eerily quiet.

I wasn't sure what the future held, but I knew I wasn't alone anymore. The road ahead would be long, with more bad days than I'd like to admit. But there was hope now—small and quiet, but real. And maybe, for now, that was enough.

The next morning, I knew what I had to do. I couldn't keep carrying this alone. The people who loved me deserved to know.

I called Lilly and asked her to meet me at our favorite coffee shop.

When she walked in and saw me sitting there, her eyes immediately narrowed. "Okay, spill. You look like someone ran you over, and I hate it." I gave her a small smile, gripping my coffee cup tighter. "I have lupus," I said, the words foreign on my tongue. "I found out a few weeks ago. I just... I didn't know how to tell you."

Lilly didn't hesitate. She stood, walked around the table, and wrapped me in a hug so tight I felt like I could finally breathe. Tears pricked my eyes as I held onto her, the weight of my secret finally lifting. We sat back down, both of us taking shaky breaths.

"I love you," she said firmly. "And I hope you know I will do everything in my power to make sure you feel that love. You deserve amazing things, Elle. This diagnosis doesn't change that."

She always knew what to say.

Telling my parents went much the same way. I went to their house for lunch, sat them down, and told them the truth.

We cried. We laughed. We reminisced about old memories. They promised to be there for me, to help however they could.

Suddenly, I didn't feel like I was holding up the weight of the world alone.

Maybe, just maybe, I didn't have to.

Chapter Twenty-Three

Things between Alex and me had been growing in ways I never expected. It wasn't just about blending our lives, our routines, our families. It wasn't just the way he had seamlessly become part of my world, present in the small, ordinary moments—making coffee in the morning, carrying Sam on his shoulders through the bookstore, laughing with Carter over some inside joke I wasn't privy to. It was something deeper. Something unspoken yet undeniably real.

At first, I resisted it.

I had convinced myself I wasn't ready. That after everything, I couldn't possibly be. My body wasn't the same. My life wasn't the same. I had scars—some visible, some buried so deep I wasn't sure they'd ever heal. How could

I expect Alex to love me fully, knowing all of it? Knowing that I came with a past that wasn't just a chapter but an entire book of struggles and survival?

But Alex, as always, was patient. He didn't rush me. He never made me feel like I was something to fix or someone to pity. He simply stood beside me, showing me—day after day—that love wasn't about being perfect. It was about being present.

The first time we kissed after fully embracing what was between us, it was different. It wasn't just passion—it was something deeper, something weightier. It was trust. It was surrender. It was the unspoken understanding that we were letting down our walls, letting each other in, fully and completely.

I had been nervous, hesitant, but Alex had sensed it before I could even put it into words. His hands had cupped my face with such tenderness that it nearly undid me, his touch a silent reassurance that he saw me—all of me. Not just the strong parts, but the ones that still trembled, the ones that still carried doubt.

And when we finally gave in to the pull between us, it wasn't just physical. It was something that wrapped around me, something that felt like home. His touch wasn't just affectionate—it was grounding. He made me feel safe in a way I hadn't realized I had been longing for.

It wasn't always easy.

Sometimes, my body betrayed me. The fatigue would settle deep in my bones, my joints aching with an unrelenting soreness I couldn't shake. But Alex never made me feel guilty for it. He adjusted without hesitation. He learned the signs—when I needed rest, when I was pretending to be fine, when I was holding back the frustration of feeling like my body had turned against me. He never once made me feel like a burden.

And that, more than anything, was what made me fall even harder.

We found a rhythm—one uniquely ours. Lazy afternoons where we didn't need words, only the quiet comfort of each other's presence. Evenings spent in whispered conversations, our fingers intertwined as we laid in bed, breathing in the stillness. There were moments filled with laughter, teasing, stolen kisses in the aisles of the bookstore. And then there were nights when he held me like I was something precious, something cherished, when every touch was unspoken reassurance that this—whatever we were building—was real.

It had been six months since we fully let ourselves fall into this, and one evening, as we laid together in bed, I felt something shift inside me. A realization. A truth I had been holding back, afraid to give voice to.

"You know," I whispered, my head resting on his chest, listening to the steady rhythm of his heartbeat, "I didn't think I could feel this way again. Not after everything."

Alex's fingers stopped their lazy path through my hair. He tilted my chin so I was looking at him, his gaze filled with an understanding that made my throat tighten.

"You don't have to explain yourself to me," he said softly, brushing his thumb over my cheek. "I get it. And I want you—all of you—no matter what."

I swallowed hard, my heart swelling with something too big to name.

"I think... I'm ready to keep giving you all of me, too."

The words weren't dramatic or grand, but they held weight. They meant that I was stepping into something I had once been too afraid to claim. That I was choosing love. Choosing him. Choosing us.

Alex smiled then, the kind of smile that made my stomach flip, and he kissed me—slowly, deeply—like he understood exactly what those words meant.

And then, barely a whisper, I let the words slip from my lips before fear could steal them back.

"I love you."

He pulled back just enough to meet my eyes. He didn't hesitate, didn't waver. He simply pressed a lingering kiss to my forehead and whispered against my skin, "I love you,

Elle. More than you can imagine. I'm not going anywhere. This thing we have—it's real. And I never want to let it go."

And just like that, something inside me settled.

I had spent so long being afraid—of losing myself, of trusting the wrong person, of loving and being left behind. But Alex had never given me a reason to doubt him. He had only ever given me reasons to believe.

I knew there would still be challenges. My illness wasn't going anywhere. Life would throw obstacles in our path. But I also knew this: What we had wasn't fleeting. It wasn't temporary.

It was steady. It was unwavering. It was love; A love I wasn't afraid to hold onto it.

Chapter Twenty-Four

It had been a few months since my lupus diagnosis, and every day felt like a quiet battle with my own body. The fatigue that had once been an occasional nuisance was now a constant companion. Some mornings, I would wake up with an aching body that seemed to move in slow motion, my joints stiff and painful. Other times, the exhaustion left me feeling as though I hadn't slept a wink despite a full night's rest.

I'd been pushing through. I *had* to. But I could feel myself wearing thin. The bookstore had always been a place I loved, but recently, every shift felt like I was dragging myself through it. I tried to make it work, but it wasn't the same anymore. There were days when I would close the store for the night and collapse on the couch, too tired to do anything else.

The thought of asking for help felt like I was admitting defeat. I was supposed to be strong and handle things on my own. I had two kids to care for, bills to pay, and a life to manage. But somewhere along the way, I realized I couldn't do it anymore.

And that's when I made the decision.

I sat on the couch one evening, Sam asleep in his bed, Carter at his father's for the weekend. Alex and I had been spending more time together, and over the last few weeks, I realized just how much he had become a part of my life. He was more than a friend, more than someone I could lean on. He was someone I was starting to *need*—not just emotionally, but physically. I couldn't do this on my own anymore.

The thought of him moving in wasn't something I had imagined when we first started dating. It felt too soon, too fast. But now, it felt like the right thing. He was steady, reliable, and always there when I needed him most. I wanted him here, in this house, with me and my boys.

It wasn't a decision I made lightly. I thought about it for days, weighing the pros and cons in my head. But in the end, it was simple. I didn't want to do this without him.

I texted Alex one evening after Sam had gone to bed. I wasn't sure how to phrase it, so I just went for it.

Hey, can we talk when you get home? It's important.

It was only a few minutes before my phone rang with Alex's name flashing across the screen. I answered quickly, trying to keep the nervousness from my voice.

"Hey, Elle. What's up?" he asked, sounding curious but calm.

"I—well, I've been thinking about something for a while now," I started, my heart racing. "I've been struggling with the lupus, and honestly, I'm just... I'm getting tired. I can't keep juggling everything. I need more help. And I think—"

I stopped myself, unsure if I was ready to say the words. But they spilled out anyway.

"I think it's time for you to move in with me. With us."

There was a long pause on the other end, and I held my breath. My heart pounded in my chest, the quiet of the room amplifying the sound. The weight of my words hung between us.

"Are you sure?" Alex finally asked, his voice softer than before, like he was trying to gauge how serious I was. "I mean, that's a big step. I've only been here a few months...

but if you're asking me to move in because you want me here, then... yeah, I think I could do that. If you need me, I'm all in."

I exhaled, the relief flooding my chest. "I do need you, Alex. I really do."

The conversation flowed easier after that. We talked logistics and the changes we'd need to make, but the most important thing was that Alex was willing to step in and be there for me how I needed him to be. I wasn't used to relying on anyone like this, but he made it easier. I could hear the smile in his voice when he said, "Alright. I'll make it work."

And that was that: a decision made, a new chapter beginning.

***

The next few days were a whirlwind of packing and moving. Alex had decided to rent out his house rather than sell it, using the extra income to help cover the expenses of his new living situation. It was practical, but it also felt like a leap of faith. He was investing in this—investing in me and my family.

It wasn't long before boxes filled the living room, and Alex was unloading his things into my space. It felt strange at first. We hadn't planned for this; it had just happened. But as the days went on, I realized how natural it felt to have him here. The space felt warmer, more alive with him in it.

But my body wasn't cooperating.

The days after Alex moved in were a blur of adjusting to the changes, both emotionally and physically. I was still dealing with the overwhelming fatigue and joint pain. Some mornings, it felt like the flu had taken over my body, and no matter how much I rested, I couldn't shake it. I had to cut back on hours at the bookstore, a decision I'd been avoiding for a while, but it was becoming clear that I couldn't keep up with everything.

"I don't know how much longer I can do this," I told Lilly one morning when I called her to catch up. "I've had to reduce my hours at the bookstore, and I don't know if that will be enough. The exhaustion's getting worse."

Lilly was quiet for a moment. I could hear the soft clink of coffee mugs in the background. "Elle, you've got to take care of yourself. I know it's hard, but you can't run yourself into the ground. You've got people around you who care. Let them help."

I could hear her concern in her voice, which made me feel guilty. I wasn't used to asking for help; now, it felt like I was asking for too much.

"I know," I sighed. "It's just hard. I'm not used to being this person. The one who can't keep up."

"You don't have to be superwoman, Elle. You're still you. I miss you. We should get together soon. John has been building a tree house. I think the boys would like it."

I smiled at that, though it was bittersweet. The idea of slowing down, of accepting that I wasn't invincible, was hard for me to wrap my head around. But deep down, I knew Lilly was right. I had to stop pretending everything was fine when it wasn't.

"Yes, Lilly, that would be nice. How about Sunday?"

"Perfect, we will see you then!" she said, and I could hear her smile on the phone.

The house was different now, with Alex's presence. It felt like a partnership, even in the little ways—making dinner together, folding laundry side by side, the quiet moments that made the days feel less isolating.

But lupus was still there, creeping in on the edges, reminding me that my body had limits. I wasn't sure how long I could keep up with the pace of life, but for now, I was taking things one day at a time, hoping that with Alex by my side, we could figure it out together.

Chapter Twenty-Five

I hadn't realized how long it had been since I had truly stepped away from my life—since I had been somewhere that didn't feel tied to my routine, my responsibilities, or the exhaustion that had become my constant companion. I couldn't remember the last time I had done something just for me, something that wasn't rooted in obligation or necessity.

When Alex suggested a vacation, my first instinct was to refuse. The idea of leaving everything behind—my children, the bookstore, my never-ending to-do list—felt impossible. Irresponsible, even. But then he said the word *Hawaii*, and something inside me hesitated. Hawaii. A place I had dreamed of visiting for as long as I could remember. The beaches, the sunsets, the rhythm of the waves crashing against the shore—it felt like another world, one I had only ever seen in photographs.

And now, suddenly, it was within reach.

"Let's do it," I said, my voice a mix of excitement and uncertainty. "Let's go to Hawaii."

The moment the words left my lips, I knew there was no turning back.

We booked our tickets that night, and just like that, something shifted. It wasn't just about the trip. It was about the *idea* of the trip—about allowing myself to step outside of my routine and simply *be*. No schedules, no responsibilities pulling at me from every direction. No carefully measured steps through a life that had started to feel too small for me.

The hardest part, however, wasn't making the decision—it was telling William. I didn't want to ask for permission. We were no longer married, and I didn't owe him explanations about my personal life. But we were co-parents, and no matter what had happened between us, our children would always be our shared priority. So, when I told him I'd be gone for a week, I braced myself for his reaction.

"Are you sure about this?" His brow furrowed, his voice careful. "Taking a trip with him while the boys are with me?"

"Yes." I met his gaze, my voice steady. "It's important. *I need this.*" There was a long pause. I could see something flicker in his expression—not quite anger, not quite disappointment. Maybe something in between. But whatever it was, he swallowed it back, nodding after a beat.

"Alright," he said finally, his tone unreadable. "The boys will be fine. They'll have a good time with me."

And just like that, the conversation was over. No argument. No passive-aggressive remarks. Just quiet acceptance. It left me feeling oddly unsettled, like I had expected more resistance, more *something* from him. But maybe this was just another reminder that we had already let go of whatever had once existed between us.

A week later, I found myself on a plane, thousands of feet above the Pacific Ocean, with Alex beside me.

The flight was long, but I didn't feel weighed down by responsibilities. There were no urgent phone calls to return, no deadlines to meet, no moody teenagers to navigate. Just the quiet hum of the airplane and the anticipation of what awaited us.

Alex and I talked for hours—about everything, about nothing. Childhood memories, places we still wanted to see, books we loved, music we listened to when we couldn't sleep. The conversation was easy, unforced. And with every passing moment, I felt lighter, like the version of me

I had been carrying for so long—the exhausted, worried, always-planning, always-sacrificing version—was slowly slipping away.

By the time we landed, something inside me had already begun to loosen.

Hawaii was more beautiful than I had imagined. The air was thick with warmth, carrying the scent of saltwater and tropical flowers. The ocean stretched endlessly before us, its surface shifting and shimmering under the sunlight, and I felt the kind of peace that didn't have to be earned or fought for. It just *was*.

We stayed in a small beachside cottage, the kind you only ever see in travel magazines—white shutters, an open veranda, a view that looked like it belonged in a painting. Every morning, I woke up to the sound of the waves, their steady rhythm lulling me into a kind of calm I hadn't known I was missing.

We spent our days exploring—walking barefoot along the shore, the sand warm and soft beneath our feet, the waves lapping at our ankles. We hiked through lush, green trails where waterfalls tumbled into hidden pools. We ate fresh seafood in open-air restaurants, the kind where no one was in a rush, where the world felt slower, easier.

But what surprised me most wasn't Hawaii itself—it was *us*.

I had expected to enjoy the trip. I had expected to feel lighter, even happy. But I hadn't expected *him* to feel like home.

There were moments when we sat in silence on the beach, side by side, the setting sun washing the sky in soft shades of pink and orange. We didn't have to talk. We didn't have to *fill* the space. It was the kind of stillness I had never experienced before—one that wasn't lonely, but comforting.

And for the first time in months, I realized I wasn't just surviving

I was *living*.

***

On our second night, after a long day of snorkeling in crystal-clear water and exploring hidden beaches, we sat on the porch of our cottage, a bottle of wine between us. The sky was endless, littered with stars, and the air was warm, carrying the scent of the ocean. Alex turned to me, his expression soft. "I'm glad we did this," he said, his voice quiet but certain.

"Me too." I smiled, looking out at the dark horizon. "I didn't realize how much I needed to escape."

He reached for my hand, threading his fingers through mine, the warmth of his touch grounding me. "I know we haven't been together long, but this..." He exhaled, shaking his head slightly. "It feels like it's been a long time coming."

I met his gaze, my chest tightening—not with fear, but with something quieter, deeper. "It does," I admitted, my voice barely above a whisper.

We sat there for a long time, neither of us in a hurry to break the moment. There was something about the ocean, about the way it stretched out endlessly, about the way it *felt* endless, that mirrored the calm I felt with him. But even here, in this paradise, my body was still mine. Lupus was still mine. The fatigue never fully left, always lurking beneath the surface. I allowed myself to forget about it for just a little while. The rest of the world could wait.

The next morning, we took a boat out to see dolphins. As I stood on the deck, the wind rushing through my hair, I thought about how different my life was now. How *different* I was.

I had spent so much of the past year in survival mode—bracing for impact, holding my breath, always waiting for something to fall apart. But now? Now, I was finally allowing myself to *be*.

The dolphins leaped beside the boat, moving effortlessly through the water, their bodies gliding in perfect synchrony with the waves. It was breathtaking, watching them move like that—so free, so unburdened.

I closed my eyes for a moment, feeling the ocean spray on my skin, the warmth of the sun on my face.

I didn't know what would come next. I didn't have all the answers. However, I wasn't afraid of the unknown. I was finally, *fully* in the moment. And right now, that was enough.

That night I sent Lilly a text message.

It is gorgeous here! Thank you so much for recommending it!

Well duh! Have you gone snorkeling yet?

I could have cried because it was so breathtaking.

I am glad you are having a blast! Tell that cutie of yours I say hello.

Chapter Twenty-Six

Our week in Hawaii passed in a blur of sunshine, saltwater, laughter, and moments that felt too good to be real. Every day was an adventure—an escape from the weight of responsibility that had been pressing on my shoulders for so long. It was as if the island itself had a way of stripping away the stress, the exhaustion, the never-ending to-do lists, leaving behind only the purest, simplest version of life.

It had been years since I had felt this free. Mornings began with the soft warmth of the sun filtering through the cottage windows, the scent of salt and hibiscus lingering in the air. Alex and I would wake slowly, tangled together in the sheets, taking our time as if the world outside didn't exist. There was no rush, no obligations—just us. And it felt... effortless.

After breakfast, we'd walk along the shoreline, the sand warm beneath our bare feet, the cool ocean breeze kissing our skin. The waves rolled in a steady rhythm, a gentle push and pull, like the pulse of the earth itself. Sometimes we talked about everything, sometimes we talked about nothing at all. But in those quiet moments, in the way he reached for my hand or tucked a stray piece of hair behind my ear, I felt a connection that went beyond words.

In the afternoons, we sought out adventure. We hiked through winding trails dense with towering palms and bright, wild orchids, the scent of fresh rain clinging to the air. We found waterfalls hidden deep in the jungle, their waters cool and crisp against our sun-warmed skin as we stood beneath the rushing falls, laughing, weightless. We kayaked through secluded bays where the water was so clear we could see the shadows of sea turtles gliding beneath us, their movements slow and deliberate, unbothered by our presence.

One afternoon, as we drifted in the middle of a quiet lagoon, the sun reflecting off the water in shimmering ribbons of gold, I sighed, resting my paddle across my lap. "Do you think we could just stay here forever?" I asked, half-joking, but also half-wishing. Alex looked over at me, his expression soft. "If it means being here with you, then yeah," he said. "No place I'd rather be."

Simple words. But they settled in my chest, anchoring something inside me. He wasn't saying it for effect, wasn't saying it because it was what I wanted to hear. He *meant* it. And I knew, without a doubt, that if I asked him to stay here with me, he would. The days passed like a dream, one moment folding seamlessly into the next. When we weren't out exploring, we spent long afternoons at the cottage, stretched out on the porch, watching the horizon shift in endless shades of blue.

We talked about the past, about the things we had lost, about the dreams we were still chasing. He told me stories about Mia, about how she had changed him, made him stronger, made him love deeper. And I told him about the version of myself I was still trying to find—the one I had lost somewhere between the divorce and the diagnosis.

But not every moment was perfect.

There were times when my body reminded me that I wasn't invincible. A sudden flare-up of pain would strike out of nowhere, my joints stiffening, my energy vanishing like a tide retreating from the shore. I hated it—the unpredictability of it, the way it snuck up on me when I least expected it, stealing time, stealing joy. But Alex never let me feel guilty for it.

When I'd wince or slow down, he'd always be there, steady as ever, his hand on my back, his voice gentle. "You don't have to do it all, Elle," he'd say, as if he could sense the frustration in me before I even spoke it. And every time, I'd exhale, letting the tension go just a little. Maybe I didn't have to be strong all the time. Maybe, for once, it was okay to let someone else share the weight.

Too soon, the trip came to an end.

The night before our flight home, we sat on the beach, watching the sun sink into the horizon, the sky burning in shades of orange, pink, and violet. The colors bled into the water, soft and infinite, reflecting everything I had felt over the past week—the beauty of slowing down, of letting go, of living without the constant weight of worry pressing into my chest.

"I don't want to leave," I admitted, my voice barely above a whisper.

Alex squeezed my hand, his thumb running slow circles against my skin. "I know," he said, his gaze fixed on the endless stretch of water before us. "It's hard to let go of something this peaceful." I leaned into him, resting my head on his shoulder, inhaling the salty air deeply as if I could somehow bottle this moment and take it home with me. "We'll come back someday, won't we?"

He turned, pressing a soft kiss to the top of my head. "We will," he promised. "As many times as you want." But no matter how many times I came back, I knew it wouldn't be the same. Because this trip, this exact moment in time, wasn't just about the destination—it was about who I was when I was here. It was about the weight I had left behind, the person I had allowed myself to become. The flight home felt different.

The reality of returning settled over me like a slow-building storm. The chaos of family life, the never-ending demands of work, the exhaustion that came with simply existing in a body that sometimes felt like my enemy—it all waited for me on the other side. Carter and Sam were with William for a few more days, giving me time to readjust before stepping back into my everyday life. But something had shifted in me. I *couldn't* just slip back into the old rhythm without acknowledging what I had learned—what Hawaii had *given* me.

I had to stop sacrificing myself for the sake of routine. I had to allow myself space to rest, to heal, to exist outside of expectations.

When Alex and I returned to my house, we stood on the porch for a moment, watching the last rays of the sunset stretch across the sky. "I'm glad we did this," I said, my voice thick with emotion. "I feel... different. Lighter."

Alex smiled, brushing a strand of hair from my face. "I feel that way too." I let out a breath, nodding. "We have to do this more often. Maybe not trips like Hawaii, but just... time for ourselves. To slow down."

Alex pulled me into a hug, holding me close. "We'll figure it out," he murmured. "Together." But no amount of preparation could have braced me for the crash that came the next morning. I woke up barely able to move. The pain was deep, radiating through every inch of me, my joints stiff and swollen, my muscles aching like I had run for miles. Alex had meetings that day, but the moment he saw me struggling, he canceled them without hesitation.

He got the boys ready for school, made breakfast, called the bookstore to let them know I wouldn't be in. He tucked me back into bed, placed heating pads around my legs, and curled up beside me, flipping through the channels until he landed on one of my favorite old sitcoms. For hours, we stayed like that—me, too exhausted to do anything but rest, and him, simply *there*.

When the boys came home, he explained to them gently that I wasn't feeling well, that tonight I wouldn't be able to play or tuck them in. Carter nodded solemnly, understanding in a way that broke my heart. Sam curled up next to me, holding my hand with his tiny fingers.

And I realized, even in my weakest moments, I wasn't alone.

I had Alex. I had my boys.

I didn't feel like I was drowning.

I had a life worth holding onto.

And I had love.

And that made all the difference.

Chapter Twenty-Seven

Life has a way of shifting when you least expect it.

For so long, it felt like I was drowning—pulled under by the weight of responsibilities, illness, uncertainty. Every day was a battle to keep my head above water, to hold everything together for my boys, for myself, for the life I was trying to rebuild. But somehow, without even realizing it, the storm had begun to settle. The chaos had given way to something steady, something manageable.

I had found my rhythm. I don't know exactly when it happened. Maybe it was the moment I finally accepted that my body had limits and started treating it with the care it deserved. Maybe it was when I stopped feeling guilty for needing rest, for saying no, for prioritizing my own well-being. The flare-ups that had once stolen so much of my life had become less frequent, less debilitating. I had learned how to listen to my body instead of fighting it, to work with it instead of punishing it for what it couldn't do.

It felt like a victory. A quiet, hard-earned victory.

And through it all, Alex had been there—steadfast, unwavering. He had seen me at my worst, on the days when I couldn't even get out of bed, when I had nothing left to give. And yet, he never faltered. He never made me feel like I was too much or not enough. He simply stayed. That kind of love was something I had never known before. But life had changed in other ways, too.

The divorce was finalized. The papers had been signed, the financial split agreed upon, and the custody arrangement set in stone. It was official. William and I were no longer bound together by marriage, only by the two boys we had promised to love and raise, no matter what.

It was bittersweet. I had spent so much time fearing this ending, wondering if I was making a mistake. But when the ink dried on the last document, all I felt was relief. A quiet kind of peace. Maybe, deep down, William had felt it too. There had been no fights, no last-minute pleadings to fix what had long since been broken. Just an understanding—spoken or unspoken—that this was what was best for all of us. And the kids? They were thriving.

Carter was navigating his teenage years with his usual sarcastic wit, still fiercely protective of his little brother, still testing boundaries in ways that both frustrated and amused me. Sam, my sweet, bright-eyed boy, had adjusted as only children can—accepting the new reality with a resilience that made my heart ache. William and I had found a way to co-exist, to co-parent without bitterness or resentment. We were no longer partners, but we were still a team where it mattered most.

And then, of course, there was Alex.

It had been a year since that first coffee date in the bookstore. A year of laughter and quiet moments. A year of adventure and learning each other's pasts. A year of falling—not just into love, but into something deeper, something lasting.

I had never expected to find this again. Not after everything.

The love I had with Alex was so different from what I had known before. It was deep, yes, but also steady, secure. There was no fear of losing myself, no pressure to be anything other than exactly who I was. It was a love built on understanding, on showing up for each other even on the hardest days. He had seen the messiest parts of me, and still, he chose to stay.

We talked about everything. Our pasts. Our fears. Our hopes for the future. One night, as we lay tangled together in bed, Alex traced slow circles on my back, his voice low and hesitant. "I've never really been sure, Elle," he admitted. "If I was ready for this. For us." I propped myself up on my elbow, searching his face. "What do you mean?" His eyes met mine, filled with quiet vulnerability. "I've loved you more than I ever thought I could after Mia. But I've been scared. Scared of moving too fast.

Scared of what it means to love someone this much again."

My chest tightened. I knew that fear. I had lived in it for so long.

But love—real love—wasn't about certainty. It was about choosing each other, even when it was terrifying. Even when the future felt uncertain. "I get it," I murmured, pressing a kiss to his shoulder. "But you don't have to have all the answers right now. We'll figure it out together." And we had.

That's why, on a crisp Saturday afternoon, standing at the top of a hill overlooking the city, I never saw it coming. We had spent the morning hiking, the trails still damp from the early morning rain. The air was cool, fresh, carrying the scent of wet earth and pine. As we reached the highest point, the view stretched out before us—rolling hills, golden in the fading autumn light, the city a distant silhouette against the sky.

It was beautiful. Quiet. Peaceful. Alex stood beside me, hands tucked into his jacket pockets, staring out at the horizon. There was something different about him, something nervous just beneath the surface. "I've been thinking a lot about us," he said, his voice steady but thick with emotion.

I turned to him, smiling. "Me too. About how much we've grown in the past year." He nodded, but there was something else in his expression—something that made my pulse quicken.

"Elle," he began, exhaling slowly, "I know we've been through a lot to get here. And I've been cautious. I've been afraid—of moving too fast, of moving forward when I wasn't sure if I could handle it. After losing Mia. After your divorce." He paused, his gaze locking onto mine. "But over the past year, I've realized I'm not afraid anymore."

My breath hitched. "What do you mean?"

His lips curled into the smallest smile, and then, before I could fully process what was happening, he reached into his jacket pocket and pulled out a small velvet box. "I love you, Elle," he said, his voice unwavering now. "I love you in a way I didn't think was possible after everything I've been through. And I want to spend the rest of my life with you. Not because I think it's the right thing to do, but because I know it's the only thing that makes sense. You're it for me. You and the boys."

My heart pounded against my ribs as he flipped open the box, revealing a simple, elegant engagement ring that caught the golden light of the setting sun. "Will you marry me?" Alex asked, his voice filled with nothing but love. For a moment, I couldn't breathe. I hadn't been expecting this. Not yet. But as I looked at him—this man who had stood beside me through every battle, who had loved me even on my hardest days—I realized something.

I *wanted* this. I *wanted* forever with him.

A tear slipped down my cheek as I whispered, "Yes."

Alex let out a breath, his relief washing over me as he slipped the ring onto my finger and pulled me into his arms. He held me so tightly, as if he never wanted to let go. "I love you," he murmured against my hair. "I love you too," I whispered back, my voice shaking but sure. "I've never been more sure of anything in my life." The past was still there—ghosts of what had been. But they no longer held me back.

This moment, this love, was my future.

And I was ready for it.

Together.

Chapter Twenty-Eight

The day of our wedding was everything I had ever hoped for—simple, intimate, and filled with the kind of love that didn't need extravagance to be meaningful. I never dreamed of a grand ceremony, of towering floral arrangements or hundreds of guests watching from polished wooden pews. I didn't need any of that. What mattered was standing beside Alex, the man who had quietly and steadily become my home, and making a promise that already felt as though it had been written into my bones.

We kept the guest list small—less than fifty people. The ones who had stood by us, through the highs and lows, through the moments of doubt and discovery. My mother, who had been my rock through my divorce and my illness.

Lilly, my best friend, who cried openly the moment she saw me in my dress, clutching my hands as if to remind me just how far I had come. And, of course, Carter and Sam, my boys, who had embraced Alex not just as someone in my life, but as someone in theirs.

It was impossible to look at them and not feel the depth of everything I had built, the new life I had created. Carter, now a teenager, held himself with that balance of quiet pride and lingering childhood awkwardness. Sam, always full of boundless energy, practically vibrated with excitement. Seeing them dressed in their little suits, their faces beaming with joy, nearly undid me before I even walked down the aisle.

The ceremony was held in a small chapel on the outskirts of town, tucked between towering oak trees and wildflowers swaying in the breeze. The weather could not have been more perfect—clear skies, sunlight filtering through the leaves, a gentle wind carrying the scent of blooming jasmine.

When the music started, my heart pounded, but not from nerves.

There was no fear, no hesitation—only the certainty that I was exactly where I was meant to be. As I walked down the aisle, my gaze locked on Alex, waiting for me at the altar. His expression was steady, calm, but full of something so raw, so open, that it nearly took my breath away. He looked at me as if I were the only thing in the world.

His suit was simple—black, elegant, understated. There were no grand gestures, no rehearsed words. Just the way he held my gaze, the way he reached for my hand the moment I stood beside him, whispering, "I love you," as if those words held the entire universe within them. And they did.

The vows were quiet, personal. They weren't about sweeping promises or grand declarations. They were about the simple, unwavering truths we had come to know about each other.

"I've spent so much of my life thinking I didn't deserve something like this," I said, my voice thick with emotion as I looked into Alex's eyes. "But I was wrong. I deserve love. I deserve to be happy. And, more than anything, I deserve *you*—the man who saw me, really saw me, and loved me anyway."

Lilly was openly sobbing in the front row. Carter and Sam, standing proudly beside us, beamed as if they understood just how much this moment meant.

When the officiant pronounced us husband and wife, the small crowd erupted into cheers, but none of it mattered in that moment. The only thing that mattered was the way Alex looked at me before he pulled me in for a kiss—a kiss that wasn't just an end to the ceremony, but a beginning. A promise.

The reception was just as simple, just as perfect.

A garden venue filled with twinkling lights and long wooden tables adorned with candles and wildflowers. There were no extravagant details, no wedding planner making sure every second went according to schedule. It was just laughter, clinking glasses, the warmth of people who loved us gathered around. And then, the dance.

Carter and Sam had been too excited to let Alex and I have the first dance alone, so they had jumped in, their hands slipping into ours as we spun around the floor. I had never felt more complete, more whole, than in that moment—our little family, moving together in time, the world narrowing down to just us.

As the night wore on, I found myself watching it all unfold from the edge of the dance floor. The way Alex leaned in to listen to my mother as she told him a story, how Sam had found his way into Lilly's arms as she twirled him around, how Carter laughed with his cousins. I had built this.

I had found love again. I had built a home within it.

But life had another surprise waiting for me.

***

A few weeks after the wedding, I was shelving books at the bookstore, the familiar scent of paper and coffee wrapping around me, when Bob and Ellen, the couple who had owned the store for years, called me into the back office. They were retiring. And they wanted *me* to take over.

At first, I didn't understand. It wasn't something I had ever considered—I had always seen myself as a part of this place, but never *owning* it. The thought felt too big, too impossible.

Bob smiled, his weathered hands resting on the desk between us. "This place has always been your second home, Elle," he said. "You've got the heart for it." Something inside me shifted.

This was it. The dream I hadn't even realized I'd been chasing. This bookstore had been my sanctuary, my escape. It had been where I had pieced myself back together after my divorce, where I had found joy again in something as simple as a well-loved novel. It was where I had met Alex. And suddenly, I knew.

"I'll do it," I said before I could overthink it, before the fear could creep in. And once the words were out, they felt right. *I'll keep it alive.* By the end of the month, the bookstore was mine.

With Alex by my side, we began to dream—about expanding, hosting events, turning it into something even more special. It wasn't just about books. It was about community. About creating a place where people could find refuge the same way I had.

It felt like everything was coming together, like every step I had taken had led me to this.

For so long, I had carried the weight of my past—my marriage, my illness, the quiet fear that I wasn't enough. But none of those things defined me anymore. *This* did. The choices I had made since. The love I had found in Alex. The home I had built with my boys. And now, I had this.

Standing in the middle of my bookstore, looking out at the life I had created, I felt something I hadn't in a long, long time.

Pride. I had made it. I had fought for this life, piece by piece, and now it was mine. As Alex walked in, a cup of coffee in one hand, his other slipping easily around my waist, he pressed a kiss to my temple. "You did it," he murmured.

"We did it," I corrected, smiling up at him. And as I stood there, surrounded by shelves of stories waiting to be read, with the love of my life beside me and a future I had built with my own two hands stretching out before me, I knew—I was exactly where I was meant to be.

Chapter Twenty-Nine

It hit me like a freight train. One day, I was standing behind the counter at the bookstore, smiling and chatting with a regular about the latest novel they had picked up. The next, my body betrayed me. It started with a dull ache in my joints, something I had learned to ignore over the years. But by the afternoon, that ache had sharpened into something unbearable. My limbs felt heavy, as though my bones had been filled with lead. Exhaustion settled over me like a thick fog, making even the simplest movements feel impossible.

I gritted my teeth and forced myself to push through the rest of the day. Customers came and went, the register beeped, the scent of freshly brewed coffee lingered in the air—but I was barely present. My fingers trembled as I counted change, my knees threatened to buckle every time I took a step.

By the time I locked up for the night, I knew.

This wasn't just a bad day. This wasn't just exhaustion from working too hard. It was a flare-up.

The kind that stole my breath, stole my mobility, stole every ounce of control I had worked so hard to regain.

By the next morning, I could barely move. The pain had settled deep into my bones, radiating from my joints like fire. My body ached in ways I hadn't felt in months, and the simple act of shifting in bed sent sharp stabs of agony through me. It felt like being trapped inside myself, like I had been locked in a body that refused to cooperate.

I couldn't make it to the bathroom without gripping the walls for support. I couldn't dress myself without wincing in pain.

I had fought so hard to regain a sense of normalcy, to convince myself that I had lupus under control. But here I was again—bedridden, helpless, and drowning in the frustration of it all.

I hated it. I hated that no matter what changes I made to my lifestyle, no matter how careful I was, lupus still had the power to knock me down whenever it pleased.

It took everything in me to reach for my phone and call Alex.

He answered on the first ring, his voice steady and familiar. "Hey, beautiful. Everything okay?"

The words caught in my throat. I didn't want to admit that I needed help. I didn't want to be *this* version of myself in front of him—the one who couldn't stand on her own, who had to rely on someone else just to get through the day.

But there was no use pretending.

"No," I whispered, my voice cracking. "I need you to come home."

That was all I had to say. He didn't ask for details. He didn't hesitate. He simply said, "I'm on my way," and hung up.

When he arrived, I was curled up in bed, surrounded by pillows, my body too weak to do anything else. He sat beside me, his eyes dark with concern, and brushed my hair from my damp forehead.

"Elle," he said softly. "You need to see the doctor. This is getting worse." Tears burned my eyes. "I know," I admitted, my voice barely above a whisper. "I hate this. I hate feeling like I'm losing control over my own body." He kissed my temple, his lips warm against my clammy skin. "You're *not* losing control," he murmured. "But you *do* need to stop trying to fight this alone."

The next morning, I made the call. My doctor squeezed me in for an emergency appointment, and even though it took every ounce of strength I had just to get out of bed, I went.

The waiting room was too bright, too sterile. The chairs were stiff, and the air smelled faintly of antiseptic. I sat there, Alex's hand wrapped around mine, trying to steady my breathing as I waited for my name to be called. When the doctor entered the exam room, he gave me a long, knowing look. He had seen me through every stage of this illness—the denial, the anger, the fight to regain control. He knew what this meant before I even said a word.

"How have you been, Elle?" he asked, his voice calm but laced with concern.

I swallowed hard. "I was doing okay," I said. "I *thought* I was managing. But then... this happened."

He nodded, his expression thoughtful. "It's common," he said. "When you finally start feeling normal again, it's easy to push yourself too hard without realizing it."

I looked away, ashamed. "I thought I could handle it. The store, the kids, *everything*. I thought I was getting better."

"You *are* getting better," he assured me gently. "But you have to understand something, Elle. Lupus doesn't *go away*. It's not something you can defeat by sheer willpower. It's always going to be part of your life, and the sooner you learn to respect your limits, the fewer setbacks you'll have."

I nodded, blinking back tears. I had spent so much time trying to *prove* something to myself—that I could still be the strong, independent woman I had always been, that I could juggle motherhood and work and love without letting lupus define me.

But maybe the real strength wasn't in pushing myself to the breaking point.

Maybe the real strength was in *accepting* that I needed help.

"You have to take a step back," my doctor continued. "For now, you need to prioritize rest. And I highly recommend hiring someone to help you run the bookstore while you recover."

The words stung more than I expected. The bookstore was *mine*. It was the thing I had built from the ground up, the thing that had given me purpose when everything else in my life had fallen apart. Handing it over—even temporarily—felt like failure.

But I *had* to do this.

If I didn't, I would never fully heal.

When I left the doctor's office, I felt a strange combination of relief and sadness. I had made the decision—I was going to let go, to take a step back, to listen to my body. It wasn't weakness. It wasn't giving up. It was just… necessary.

Alex was already making adjustments at home, picking up more responsibilities without hesitation. But I needed someone at the bookstore, too.

A few days later, I hired Rachel—a former assistant manager from another shop in town. She was smart, passionate, and, most importantly, she understood how much the bookstore meant to me. She wasn't there to *replace* me. She was there to help me keep my dream alive while I gave myself the time to heal.

At first, it was hard. Staying home while someone else took over my duties felt foreign. But as the days stretched on, I began to understand something I had spent years ignoring—*I wasn't invincible.*

I *needed* rest. I *needed* to slow down. And that was okay.

> Don't you worry about a thing Elle. Things at the store are going just fine.

> Yes, that shipment came in but one of the boxes with a new release was damaged.

> Oh no. Don't send it back. Send me some pictures and we can decide if we just want to do a sale on them.

> Sounds good. They aren't in bad shape since they are hard cover but we just weren't prepared for it.

One afternoon, as I lay in bed, the soft glow of sunlight filtering through my bedroom window, I realized something: this was just another part of my journey. Another challenge. Another test of resilience. I had survived heartbreak. I had survived divorce. I had survived the worst of my illness before, and I would survive this, too. Lupus didn't own me. It never would. This flare-up wasn't the end of my story. It was just a temporary setback.

And when I was ready, I would rise again. Because that's who I was.

A fighter.

Chapter Thirty

Life with Alex and the boys under one roof was an adventure—both exhilarating and challenging. There were moments of pure, unfiltered joy. Laughter echoed around the dinner table as Sam told one of his exaggerated stories, waving his hands wildly while Carter rolled his eyes but couldn't quite hide his smile. Saturday afternoons turned into lazy, movie-watching marathons, all of us tangled up on the couch under a shared blanket, the scent of popcorn lingering in the air. Mornings were filled with the familiar sounds of cereal bowls clinking, sleepy grumbles, and the occasional rush to find missing homework or misplaced shoes.

This—this feeling of home, of belonging—was what I had hoped for when Alex moved in. But even in the midst of happiness, there were growing pains. Merging two separate lives into one wasn't seamless. It was an adjustment, a learning curve filled with unspoken habits and small, unintentional clashes. I had spent years running my household in a particular way, managing the boys, handling responsibilities, setting routines that worked for us. Now, there was another adult in the mix—someone with his own methods, his own instincts.

Alex and I had found an easy rhythm as a couple, but as co-parents? That was new territory. Carter and Sam were excited about the change, but that didn't mean they weren't still processing it. Having Alex here full-time wasn't the same as him visiting for dinner or spending the weekend. He was *here*. Present in every moment, part of their everyday lives. He wasn't their father, and he never tried to be. But even without that expectation, the transition wasn't effortless.

One of the first challenges came on a Monday morning, three weeks after Alex moved in. The weekend had been a blur of bookstore events and errands, and I had been running on empty. That morning, I was already late picking up Sam from daycare, my body aching from pushing too hard. In the living room, I could hear the boys bickering—voices escalating, frustration rising. "Mom, Carter's not letting me play with the toy car!" Sam's voice carried down the hall, laced with impatience.

"You have to share, Sam!" Carter shot back, his tone just as stubborn.

"I *was* playing first!" Sam shouted, and I could hear the telltale sounds of a struggle over the toy. I exhaled, rubbing my temple. I didn't have time to referee. My arms were full—keys, phone, purse, the weight of the day pressing down on me.

"Alex!" I called toward the other room, my voice edged with urgency. "Can you help them? I'm running late!"

He appeared in the doorway, eyebrows raised, caught mid-task. But when he saw the stress written across my face, he simply nodded. "I got it, Elle. Don't worry." I hesitated for half a second, my instinct screaming to intervene, to handle it myself. But I pushed past it and rushed out the door. The whole drive to daycare, the knot in my stomach remained. It wasn't about whether Alex was capable—I *knew* he was. But trusting someone else with the everyday battles, with the little moments of discipline and teaching? That was harder than I expected.

When I returned home that evening, I braced myself for chaos.

Instead, I walked in to find Sam curled up in Alex's lap, both of them racing toy cars across the coffee table. Laughter filled the room, the earlier argument long forgotten. A small victory. I exhaled slowly, realizing that this was part of the process—learning to let go, to let him step in, to share the weight of this life we were building together. But the biggest challenge wasn't in the little moments. It was in the realization that I *couldn't* do everything anymore.

Even with my lupus relatively stable, the exhaustion never fully left me. Some days, it crashed over me without warning, leaving me drained, unable to move at the pace I once had. I had spent years handling it all—being the mother, the provider, the one who picked up the pieces no matter how tired or overwhelmed I was. But now, with Alex here, the balance was shifting.

He took over without hesitation, helping where he could, stepping in when I couldn't. And while I *should* have been grateful, I found myself wrestling with guilt.

One evening, after dinner, I sat on the couch, watching him clear the plates while the boys played nearby. I *should* have been up, helping. But I wasn't. I *couldn't*. I sighed, running a hand through my hair. "Alex, I feel like I'm not pulling my weight."

He turned, drying his hands, then crossed the room to sit beside me.

"Elle," he said gently, his voice filled with warmth. "You're going through a lot. And I *want* to help. This isn't about keeping score—it's about being partners." I shook my head, frustration bubbling beneath my exhaustion. "But you didn't sign up for this. For me being—" I gestured vaguely, struggling to find the words. "*Like this.*"

His expression softened. "I vowed to love you in sickness and in health, remember? That wasn't just something I *said*. I meant it."

I swallowed the lump in my throat. "I just don't want you to feel stuck."

"I don't feel stuck," he assured me. He lifted my chin so I had to meet his eyes. "I feel like I'm exactly where I'm meant to be."

His words settled deep in my chest, easing the burden I had been carrying. He was right. I wasn't failing. I wasn't a burden. I was *fighting*—for my health, for my family, for the life we were creating. Even if I couldn't always do it all, that didn't mean I wasn't still part of this.

And the boys? They were adjusting in their own ways.

Sam, ever the affectionate one, had begun seeking Alex out after school, asking him to play, to read stories, to help build elaborate Lego towers in the living room. Carter, though, was a different story. He was distant—not outright defiant, but reserved. He kept his interactions with Alex short, his walls still firmly in place.

One evening, after Carter brushed off another attempt from Alex to help with his math homework, I found him curled up in his bed, staring at the ceiling.

"Hey, bud," I said, sitting on the edge of the mattress. "Wanna talk?" He hesitated, then sighed. "I don't *hate* Alex, Mom." His voice was quiet. "I just don't like how everything's changing. I miss how things used to be." My heart clenched. I *knew* this adjustment wasn't easy, but hearing it from him—hearing the sadness behind his words—hit me harder than I expected.

"I get it," I admitted, brushing his hair back like I used to when he was younger. "Change is *hard*. And I'm not asking you to love this right away. I just need you to know that Alex isn't here to take anything away from you. He's here because I love him. And because he loves us." Carter didn't respond right away, but after a long pause, he gave a small nod. "Okay." It wasn't an instant fix. It wasn't a perfect resolution. But it was *something*.

By the end of the month, the rough edges of our new life had started to smooth out. There were still bumps, still moments of tension and adjustment, but there was also *growth*. There was laughter. There was love.

And as I sat on the couch one Sunday afternoon, watching Carter—hesitant but willing—lean into Alex's side as they flipped through a book together, I knew we were getting there.

It wasn't perfect. But it was ours and it was so beautiful.

Chapter Thirty-One

As we continued learning how to live together as a blended family, it became clear that there was no one-size-fits-all solution. No handbook could prepare us for the daily adjustments, the unspoken tensions, or the small triumphs that made this new life both challenging and beautiful. Each day was an experiment—a mix of trial and error, laughter and frustration, new habits and growing pains. We had to carve out space for one another, adjust expectations, and, most importantly, never stop communicating.

Some days felt like an uphill battle.

Like when Carter refused to go to his dad's for the weekend because he didn't want to leave a project he and Alex had been working on—a model airplane that had become their shared labor of love. I could see the conflict in Carter's eyes, torn between his loyalty to his father and his growing connection with Alex.

"You can finish it when you get back," I told him gently, trying to reassure him. But his brow furrowed, frustration simmering beneath his words. "It won't be the same." I knew what he meant. I knew this was more than a model airplane; it was about the time he had spent with Alex, the quiet moments they were finally starting to build together. But I also knew that keeping balance—keeping a connection with William—was just as important. It wasn't easy to navigate, and it wasn't something I had an answer for. We were still figuring it out.

Then there were the unexpected, heart-wrenching moments—like when Sam, small and innocent, looked up at me one night with those wide, earnest eyes and asked, "Why can't Alex be my *real* dad?" The question caught me off guard, stealing the air from my lungs. He wasn't asking in a way that dismissed William—he was just trying to make sense of his little world, to understand why the man who tucked him into bed at night, who played trains with him on the living room floor, who made pancakes in the shape of dinosaurs on Saturday mornings—wasn't the one who had always been there.

I knelt beside him, brushing a hand through his soft curls. "Alex loves you so much, bud. You don't have to share the same last name for him to be a real part of your life." He thought about that for a long moment, his tiny fingers tracing patterns on his blanket. "But he *feels* like my dad." Tears burned at the corners of my eyes, but I swallowed them back. I kissed the top of his head, holding him close. "That's because family isn't just about where we come from. It's about who shows up, who loves us, and who stays."

That seemed to satisfy him, at least for now. But for me, it was another reminder of how complicated blending our lives had become. There were no easy answers—only moments of love and patience, of navigating the in-between spaces and learning to make them our own. Still, in the midst of the struggles, there were moments of pure, undeniable joy—reminders of why we were doing this.

One crisp autumn afternoon, Alex and Carter spent the entire day working in the backyard, hammering and sawing, their heads bent in quiet concentration as they built a treehouse in the massive oak tree. It had started as an idea—a casual suggestion inspired by Lilly and John's treehouse—but now, it was becoming something real, something ours.

Sam ran circles around them, already planning his first adventure, even though it was far from finished.

"Can we make it a pirate ship?" he asked, eyes wide with excitement. "And put a flag on top? And a secret trapdoor?"

Alex laughed, wiping sawdust from his hands. "I like the way you think, kid."

Carter, though less outwardly enthusiastic, was absorbed in the process. He measured carefully, mimicking the way Alex worked, his hesitation slowly being replaced with confidence. I watched from the kitchen window, my heart full as I saw them working side by side—the quiet understanding that had begun to build between them evident in the way they communicated without words.

Later that evening, after the tools had been put away and the last of the golden daylight faded into dusk, I stood in the doorway and watched them from afar. Alex had an arm draped around Carter's shoulders, and Sam was tugging on his hand, still chattering about pirate names. The sound of their laughter filled the space around me, warm and effortless.

This was what we were building—something real, something solid. That night, as we climbed into bed, I turned to Alex, my head resting on his shoulder. "Did you see Carter today?" I murmured. "The way he was looking at you while you were working together?" Alex exhaled, running a hand through my hair. "Yeah," he said softly. "I think he's starting to trust me."

I nodded, tracing small circles on his chest. "You're patient with him. You don't push. That means everything."

He kissed the top of my head. "They mean everything to me."

Each day brought its own challenges, but Alex showed me—over and over again—that we were a team. That I didn't have to carry this all on my own. He showed it in the quiet ways.

In the way he helped Carter with his math homework before dinner, never growing frustrated even when Carter struggled.

In the way he sat on the floor with Sam, building elaborate train tracks, making exaggerated train noises just to hear him laugh.

In the way he researched early learning programs and printed out kindergarten-level worksheets, teaching Sam basic reading skills at the kitchen table, his voice gentle and patient.

He wasn't just a man who had stepped into our lives. He was *choosing* us, every single day. And as I lay there in the quiet of our home, listening to the distant hum of the boys talking in their rooms, I felt something settle deep inside me—a peace I hadn't known I needed. We weren't perfect, but were becoming a family.

And that? That was everything.

Chapter Thirty-Two

L ife had been moving forward in fits and starts. The moments of quiet normalcy were beginning to surface more often, but they were hard-won. Our family—this carefully woven, delicate thing we were building—was beginning to find its balance. But the balance was fragile, easily disrupted by the smallest shift. Some days, it felt like we had settled into something steady, like we had figured out how to move together in this new life. And then, without warning, something would tilt, and I would feel like I was right back at the beginning, trying to piece everything together.

But the one thing that remained constant—the one thing I could hold onto when everything else felt uncertain—was that I was learning to be vulnerable in ways I had never allowed myself before. Alex and I had fallen into an easy rhythm, sharing the responsibilities of the house, the boys, and everything in between. We were a team, dividing the weight between us. It should have felt like a relief, and in many ways, it did. But I couldn't ignore the parts of me that still held onto the need for control—the parts of me that still felt guilty for letting him carry so much.

Carter was adjusting, though I could tell he still held some quiet reservations. He was growing older, stepping into his teenage years, and I knew he was trying to define himself within a family dynamic that had shifted beneath him. He liked Alex—he had even started coming to him for help with things he wouldn't have asked before—but there was still a distance there, something unspoken that neither of us knew how to bridge just yet.

Sam, on the other hand, was eager, affectionate, and full of questions. He didn't see the complications in any of it, only that Alex was there—helping him tie his shoes, praising his drawings, carrying him to bed when he fell asleep on the couch. To him, Alex was as much a part of our family as anyone else.

And yet, despite the progress we were making, there were days when the weight of it all—the changes, the responsibilities, the expectations—pressed down on me, making it hard to breathe. And then there were the days when my body reminded me that no matter how much I wanted to hold everything together, I couldn't always control the way things unfolded.

***

It started on a Monday morning.

The weekend had been full—errands, homework, a trip to the bookstore, and a rare evening of laughter as we all sat together on the couch, watching a movie. It had felt good. It had felt normal. But when I opened my eyes that morning, I knew something was wrong. The first thing I noticed was the heaviness, a deep, bone-deep fatigue that made it impossible to lift my limbs. Then, the pain—sharp and unrelenting, radiating from my joints as if my own body were turning against me.

I tried to sit up, but my arms gave out beneath me. My breath came in shallow gasps. It was happening again. The lupus flare had been creeping up on me for days, a quiet warning that I had ignored, convincing myself that I could push through it. But now, there was no pushing through. There was only the cruel reminder that my body had limits I couldn't negotiate with.

Alex had left early for work, and I was alone in the house with the boys still asleep down the hall. I tried to swing my legs over the edge of the bed, but the effort sent a sharp pain up my spine.

Panic set in as I realized I couldn't even stand, let alone take care of the morning routine. I reached for my phone, staring at it for too long before finally unlocking the screen. I hated this part—relying on someone else, asking for help when I had spent so much of my life proving that I could handle things on my own. But the truth was undeniable. I couldn't do it alone today.

My fingers trembled as I typed the message to Alex:

> I need help. I can't get out of bed.

The reply came faster than I expected.

> I'm coming home. Hang in there. I'll be right there.

The relief hit me like a wave, but beneath it was something heavier—something I wasn't ready to face yet. The realization of just how much I had been holding back. How much I had been afraid to admit, not just to Alex but to myself. When he walked through the front door, he was quiet, careful not to wake the boys. He made his way to me without hesitation, sitting beside me on the bed. His eyes were filled with concern, his touch gentle as he brushed a strand of hair from my face.

"Hey," he murmured. "How are you doing?"

I exhaled shakily. "Not good," I admitted. "I hate feeling like this. I hate that I can't even get up."

He didn't hesitate. "Elle, you don't have to do this alone," he said, his voice steady but full of warmth. "You're not weak for needing help."

The words hit me harder than I expected, and before I could stop myself, the tears came. I wasn't just crying for today—I was crying for everything. For the exhaustion of always fighting to be strong. For the frustration of living in a body that betrayed me when I needed it most. For the guilt of feeling like I was failing the people who depended on me.

Alex didn't try to fix it. He didn't rush me to stop or tell me it was going to be okay. He just pulled me into his arms, holding me as I let it all out.

"It's okay to need help," he whispered into my hair. "You've been so strong, but you don't always have to be. I'm here. I'll always be here."

And in that moment, I believed him.

The next few days passed in a haze of rest and recovery. Alex took over everything—getting the boys to school, making dinner, handling the bookstore when he could.

I had never let anyone take control like that before, not even when I was married to William. I had always carried the weight of everything, believing that if I let go, even for a moment, everything would fall apart. But now, I was learning—slowly, painfully—that leaning on someone else didn't make me weak.

That night, when the boys were in bed, Alex sat with me on the couch, his fingers tracing slow, absentminded circles against my skin. "I need to be honest with you about something," he said after a long pause. I turned to him, sensing the weight in his words. "What is it?" He took a breath, his gaze steady. "I love you, Elle. And I'm not going anywhere. But I need you to take care of yourself. I need you to let me help. Because I can't stand watching you push yourself to the point where you break."

I swallowed hard, my chest tightening. "I don't mean to push myself," I whispered. "I just... I don't know how to do it any other way."His hands cupped my face, his touch firm but full of warmth. "Then let's figure it out together," he said. "You don't have to carry everything alone."

The words settled deep, anchoring me in a way I hadn't felt before. I had spent so long believing that my strength was in how much I could endure. But maybe real strength was in allowing myself to be loved, to be cared for. To believe I was worthy of it.

I closed my eyes, leaning into him. "Okay," I whispered. "I'll try."

And it was in that moment, I let myself breathe.

Chapter Thirty-Three

The days had been slipping through my fingers faster than I could keep up with, each one vanishing before I could truly grasp it. Life had a way of moving forward whether I was ready for it or not, and I often found myself standing at the crossroads between what was and what could be.

Sometimes, I could still hear the echoes of my old life—the one before everything changed. The life where I thought I had all the answers, where I believed in things like certainty and forever.

But then, of course, there were the things I never saw coming.

Like Alex. Like the bookstore. Like the unexpected beauty of learning to live again when I had once thought my story was over.

In the past year, I had learned so much—more than I ever could have imagined back when I was still trapped in the cycle of my old life. I had learned that healing wasn't just about time passing; it was about allowing myself to feel—to truly feel. To sit in the discomfort of my own emotions, to acknowledge the pain and grief instead of running from them. And in doing so, I had also learned that even in the darkest moments, there was light to be found.

Most importantly, I had learned that love—the kind of love that truly matters—could be found in the places I least expected.

It was a Wednesday afternoon when it happened. I was curled up on the couch, watching the boys play their video games. Carter was deep in concentration, his jaw set in that familiar way he had when he was focused, while Sam giggled at every little thing happening on the screen. The warmth of the house, the sound of their laughter—it should have felt like an ordinary day.

But something was off.

A wave of exhaustion rolled through me, sudden and forceful, knocking the breath from my lungs. It was the kind of exhaustion that didn't come from lack of sleep but from something deeper—something that had been lurking beneath the surface, waiting for its moment to strike. My body felt heavy, my limbs sluggish, as though I were moving through thick, invisible molasses.

I tried to ignore it, pushing the feeling down. I wasn't just tired—I knew that. It was the familiar warning of an oncoming lupus flare, a quiet but insistent reminder that my illness was always there, waiting for the slightest excuse to remind me of its presence.

I stood up, determined to shake it off, but the moment I did, the room swayed. My knees buckled, and I had to grab onto the couch to keep myself upright. A sharp pang of fear shot through me as dizziness wrapped itself around my senses. My heart pounded in my chest. I squeezed my eyes shut, willing the sensation to pass.

"Mom?" Carter's voice cut through the fog, sharp with concern. He was standing beside me now, his eyes scanning my face.

I forced a small smile, hoping to reassure him. "I'm fine," I said, though my voice came out softer than I intended. "Just a little dizzy."

Carter didn't look convinced. "Maybe you should lie down."

I nodded, swallowing the lump forming in my throat. "I will. Thanks for checking in." Sam, who had been engrossed in his game, suddenly looked up and ran over, his small hand reaching for mine. "Mom, you okay?" His voice was full of worry, his brown eyes wide and searching.

I knelt down, forcing myself to steady my breath. "I'm okay, buddy," I reassured him, squeezing his tiny fingers. "Just a little tired." He seemed to accept my answer, giving me a quick nod before running back to his game. But Carter lingered, his gaze flickering between me and the hallway leading to my bedroom.

"You should rest," he said quietly. I knew he was right.

With slow, deliberate steps, I made my way to the bedroom, every movement feeling heavier than the last. The second I curled up beneath the blankets, I knew I wasn't going anywhere for a while. My body wasn't giving me a choice.

I hated this part. The part where I had to stop. The part where I had to acknowledge that no matter how much I wanted to keep up—to be the mother, the business owner, the partner I wanted to be—I couldn't always outrun my own limitations.

When Alex came home, I was still in bed, the weight of exhaustion pressing me down. I heard his footsteps in the hallway before he appeared in the doorway, his brow furrowed in concern. "Elle?" His voice was soft but urgent as he crossed the room and sat beside me. "The boys told me you almost fell over." I exhaled slowly, keeping my gaze fixed on the ceiling. "Just a little dizzy," I murmured. "I think I pushed too hard again."

Alex studied me for a moment before shaking his head, his expression equal parts frustration and love. "You've been doing too much, haven't you? You can't keep running yourself into the ground like this. You need to rest. You need to let me help."

I closed my eyes, the guilt rising inside me like a tide. "I don't know how to stop," I admitted. "There's so much to do. If I sit down, it won't get done."

Alex reached for my hand, his fingers warm and steady around mine. "Elle, you have a village behind you. You have me. You have Rachel at the bookstore, your parents helping with the boys. You don't have to do it all alone. You *shouldn't* do it all alone."

Tears pricked at my eyes before I could stop them. "I don't want to let anyone down," I whispered.

"You won't," he said, squeezing my hand. "Not with me by your side. You don't have to carry this alone." The next morning, I made an appointment with my doctor. I knew I couldn't keep going like this—not if I wanted to have a future with the people I loved. Sitting in the doctor's office, the sterile scent of antiseptic filling the air, I felt the familiar sense of unease settle in my chest. I hated these conversations, hated admitting how much lupus still controlled my life. But as I spoke, explaining the dizziness, the fatigue, the overwhelming need to keep pushing forward, I realized something.

This wasn't a sign of weakness.

This was strength.

I wasn't giving up—I was choosing to fight smarter.

My doctor listened carefully, nodding in understanding before offering me the advice I already knew deep down but had refused to accept.

"You need to slow down, Elle. Your body is telling you it's time to make a change."

The words were hard to hear, but I nodded, feeling a mix of relief and fear flood my chest. "What do I need to do?"

She gave me a steady look. "First, you need to cut back your hours at the bookstore. I know how much it means to you, but you need to let Rachel take on more responsibility. You also need to prioritize your health—better sleep, better balance, and, most importantly, less stress."

The words settled deep within me. I had been here before, receiving this same advice, but this time felt different. This time, I wasn't just hearing them—I was ready to listen.

When I returned home, I sat down with Alex and the boys. I told them everything. The doctor's advice, the changes I needed to make, the fact that I couldn't keep doing things the way I had been.

"We're a team," Alex said, wrapping his arm around me. "And we'll figure it out together."

And just like that, I knew.

This wasn't the end of something. This wasn't about giving up. This was about choosing to live—to truly live.

I didn't want to just survive anymore.

I wanted to be here.

For Alex. For the boys.

For myself.

Chapter Thirty-Four

The days had started to feel more manageable. The worst of my lupus flare had passed, and I found myself moving through the world without feeling like my body was betraying me at every turn. I was still learning how to embrace a slower pace of life—to listen when my body told me to rest instead of pushing through out of habit. It wasn't always easy, and the guilt still crept in when I least expected it, but I was learning. And Alex was there, steady as always, by my side.

It was a Monday morning, the kind that carried the promise of an ordinary day, when I found myself at the kitchen table, fingers wrapped around a warm mug of tea. The scent of chamomile filled the air as I watched Sam and Carter argue over the last muffin.

"It's mine!" Sam declared, his little hands clutching the plate as Carter tried to wrestle it from him.

"You already had one," Carter countered, giving him a look of pure older-brother authority. "You don't even like blueberry."

Sam scowled, puffing out his chest. "I do today!"

I smirked, sipping my tea as Alex moved between them with the practiced ease of a man who had learned the art of refereeing sibling disputes. "Alright, boys. Let's solve this fairly. Rock, paper, scissors."

Carter rolled his eyes but held out his fist. Sam, thrilled at the prospect of battle, eagerly followed. Within seconds, the game was over—Carter's rock crushed Sam's scissors.

"Fine," Sam grumbled, crossing his arms. "But I still think I should have won." Alex ruffled his hair before tossing Carter the muffin. "Good effort, kid."

As I sat there, watching the playful exchange, I felt something settle deep in my chest. It wasn't just contentment—it was something more profound. The kind of peace that comes not from everything being perfect, but from knowing that, despite the imperfections, everything was exactly as it should be.

The phone rang, jolting me from my thoughts. I glanced at the screen, my eyebrows lifting when I saw the name of the bookstore's accountant.

"Hello?" I answered, shifting my mug to my other hand.

"Hi, Elle. It's Maria. I just wanted to give you a quick update. The bookstore's finances are looking great. You're hitting all your targets, and there's even been an increase in sales this month. I know things have been tough, but the changes you've made seem to be paying off."

A slow smile spread across my face. There had been so many moments of doubt—moments where I wondered if I had taken on too much, if I had made a mistake in buying the store. But this—this was proof that I had been right to believe in it.

"That's amazing," I said, letting out a breath I hadn't realized I was holding.

Maria continued, her voice warm. "I've been hearing from some of your regulars. They love the new layout and the events you've been hosting. It's really creating a great atmosphere in there."

My heart swelled. It had never just been about selling books for me. It had been about creating a place where people felt at home, where stories weren't just purchased but shared.

"Thank you," I said sincerely. "That means everything."

After we finished our conversation, I set the phone down and looked across the kitchen. Alex was clearing the plates, stealing sips from his coffee, while Carter and Sam had already moved on to something else, their argument over the muffin forgotten.

He must have felt my gaze because he turned, raising a questioning brow. "Good news?"

"Yeah," I said, my smile lingering. "The bookstore's doing great. We're finally finding our stride."

He walked over, placing his hand on my shoulder. "I'm proud of you, Elle. You've worked so hard for this."

I looked up at him, something tender and unspoken passing between us. "I couldn't have done it without you. You've made all the difference."

Alex's expression softened, and for a moment, it felt as though the rest of the world had faded away. There was no rush, no weight to carry, just us—building something beautiful together.

The rest of the morning passed quickly. I spent time reading over inventory reports while the boys played outside. Alex, ever patient, helped Carter with his latest science project while Sam busied himself collecting rocks and sticks, a grand adventure unfolding in his min

It was all so simple. But it was real. And it was everything I had ever wanted. By the afternoon, I felt the familiar pull of exhaustion creeping in—not the bone-deep kind that came with a flare-up, but the kind that came from a full day well spent. I stretched my arms overhead, letting out a sigh before making my way into the kitchen, where Alex was chopping vegetables for dinner.

"Alex?" I called, watching as he skillfully worked the knife across the cutting board.

"Yeah?" He glanced up, flashing me that easy grin that still managed to make my heart skip a beat.

"I was thinking about something."

He wiped his hands on a dish towel, turning to face me with a knowing smirk. "Something good or something bad?"

"Something good," I assured him, my smile widening. "What do you think about us going away for the weekend? Just the two of us. We've been so focused on everything—I think we deserve a little break."

His eyes softened, and for a brief moment, I saw something deeper flicker across his expression. Not just excitement, but something more. Something like understanding. Like peace.

"I think that sounds like exactly what we need," he said quietly.

We settled on a weekend getaway—a small cabin by the lake, somewhere quiet, where we could just be. No distractions. No obligations. Just time to breathe, to be together.

As we drove away from the city, the road stretching endlessly before us, I felt something inside me begin to loosen. For so long, I had been carrying everything—my illness, my responsibilities, my fears—so tightly, afraid that if I let go even a little, everything would fall apart. But now, with Alex's hand resting on my knee, the hum of the radio filling the space between us, I realized that maybe letting go wasn't the same as losing control.

Maybe it was just another way of trusting that everything would be okay. When we arrived at the cabin, it was everything I had hoped for—quiet, simple, and breathtakingly beautiful. We spent the evening sitting on the porch, watching the sunset paint the lake in strokes of orange and pink, the water shimmering like liquid gold.

"Elle," Alex said after a long silence, his voice steady and sure. "I know we've been through a lot—more than I ever imagined. But I want you to know that I'm here. I'm here for all of it."

I turned to him, my heart swelling at the quiet certainty in his words.

"I know," I whispered. "And I'm here for you, too."

As the sky darkened and the stars blinked into existence above us, I let myself believe it.

Chapter Thirty-Five

It's strange how time works—how it stretches and contracts, how the past can feel both distant and impossibly close. Days blur into weeks, weeks into months, and before you realize it, an entire year has passed. I used to believe that time alone was enough to heal wounds, that distance from pain would somehow erase it. But I've learned that healing isn't about forgetting—it's about remembering differently.

Some memories have faded into soft echoes, their edges no longer sharp. Others—the important ones—have etched themselves into the very core of who I am, shaping me in ways I never expected.

A year ago, I was living in survival mode, clinging to a version of life that no longer fit me. I was exhausted—physically, emotionally—trapped in a cycle of fear, loss, and uncertainty. I had no idea how to move forward, no idea that something beautiful was waiting on the other side of the chaos.

And then, there was Alex. There was the bookstore. There was the slow, steady realization that life wasn't just about getting through the day—it was about living. Really living.

I had faced so much in the past year—pain, loss, the weight of chronic illness—but I had also found joy, connection, and, most surprisingly, a quiet kind of peace.

The boys were thriving. Carter had settled into his teenage years with fewer outbursts and more thoughtful conversations. He still had moments of frustration, but he had grown in ways that made me so proud. Sam, my little ball of endless energy, had found in Alex something steady—someone to teach him, to guide him, to be the kind of presence I had always hoped he would have.

We weren't just figuring things out anymore. We were living them.

Alex and I had learned the dance of a blended family—the delicate balance of giving and taking, of knowing when to step in and when to step back. It wasn't seamless. There were moments of tension, of growing pains, of unspoken fears that still surfaced from time to time. But there was also laughter. There were the small, quiet moments that made all of it worth it. We had built something together—imperfect but solid, a life that felt like home.

And as for my lupus—it had become a chapter in my story, but it no longer defined me. I had learned how to manage it, how to listen to my body instead of fighting against it. There were still difficult days, still moments when exhaustion pulled me under, but I no longer saw them as failures. I knew, without a doubt, that I didn't have to face them alone anymore. That was the greatest lesson of all—not just that I needed help, but that accepting it didn't make me weak. It made me whole.

That Tuesday morning, I stood in front of the large windows of the bookstore, watching the city wake up beyond the glass. The early sun filtered through the trees, spilling golden light across the sidewalk. It was still quiet inside, just the way I liked it. I had spent the morning catching up on emails, reorganizing the shelves, and breathing in the familiar scent of ink and paper.

The bell above the door chimed, pulling me from my thoughts.

Lilly walked in, her presence as vibrant as ever, her laughter filling the space before she even spoke. She moved through the store like she belonged there, which, in a way, she always had.

"I was wondering when I'd see you today," she teased, leaning against the counter. "How's life?"

I exhaled, letting my hands rest on the wooden surface. "It's good," I said honestly. "Really good."

Lilly narrowed her eyes, crossing her arms. "That's it? Just 'good'?"

I chuckled, shaking my head. "Okay, fine. It's better than good. The bookstore is thriving, more than I ever expected it would. My health is stable. The kids are adjusting. Alex and I—" I paused, the words settling over me. "We've built something together. It's not perfect, but it feels right. I feel like... I'm really living for the right reasons, you know?"

Lilly's expression softened, a quiet kind of pride in her eyes. "I love seeing you like this," she said. "You've fought so hard for this life. And you did it, Elle. You built something beautiful."

Her words landed deep, wrapping around the parts of me that had once doubted I'd ever get here.

"I couldn't have done it without you," I said, my voice softer now. "You were there for me when I couldn't see the way forward. You've always been my anchor."

Lilly smiled, reaching across the counter to squeeze my hand. "That's what friends are for."

The bell rang again, and a young woman walked in, holding a book in her hands.

"Hi," she said, her voice a little hesitant. "I was wondering if you had any recommendations for a good mystery novel?"

I straightened, my smile widening. "Of course. What kind of mysteries do you like?"

As I guided her through the shelves, sharing my favorite recommendations, I felt it again—that quiet certainty that this was exactly where I was meant to be. This bookstore, my bookstore, wasn't just a business. It was a place of connection, of stories shared and discovered. It was a piece of my heart woven into something real.

Later that evening, after the boys had gone to bed, I sat at the kitchen table with Alex, the hum of the house settling into the kind of comfortable quiet that only came at the end of the day.

"How are you feeling?" he asked, his voice steady as he studied me from across the table.

I took a deep breath, the kind that made my lungs expand fully, the kind that didn't feel rushed or heavy.

"I'm good," I said. "Better than good, actually. I've been thinking a lot about everything lately. About how much has changed."

Alex nodded, a small smile tugging at his lips. "I can tell. You seem... lighter."

"I am," I admitted, warmth flooding through me. "I spent so long waiting for life to be easier, waiting for the hard parts to disappear. But now, I think I finally understand that it's not about things being easy. It's about knowing you can handle them when they're hard."

Alex reached across the table, taking my hand in his. "And you're not handling them alone anymore."

I squeezed his fingers, the truth of his words settling deep inside me. "I know." The next few days passed in a blur of normalcy—grocery runs, bookstore events, lazy afternoons spent curled up with the boys watching movies. Life no longer felt chaotic. It was steady, grounded in love and intention.

One evening, as the sun dipped below the horizon, painting the sky in streaks of pink and gold, Alex and I sat on the porch, a blanket wrapped around my shoulders. The crickets hummed their familiar tune, and the air carried the crisp promise of a new season. "We've been through a lot," Alex murmured beside me.

I smiled, resting my head against his shoulder. "We sure have."

"But we made it," he said, his arm wrapping around me, pulling me closer. "Together."

I let my eyes drift closed, listening to the steady rhythm of his heartbeat. "Yeah," I whispered. "We really have."

And in that moment, I knew—this wasn't just an ending.

It was a beginning.

Our beginning.

Chapter Thirty-Six

The air was crisp with the first whispers of autumn, carrying the scent of fallen leaves and the faint aroma of coffee from the shop down the street. I stood outside the bookstore, my arms wrapped around myself, watching as the sun dipped below the horizon. The golden light stretched long shadows across the pavement, painting everything in the soft glow of a season on the cusp of change.

I had stood in this exact spot countless times before, my feet firmly planted, watching the world move around me. This moment should have felt familiar. Routine. But today, everything felt different. Today, I could feel the closing of a chapter, the shift of something greater than myself.

The past had finally settled behind me, and the future was stretching out before me, waiting.

One year.

One year since Alex and I had said our vows, promising to walk forward together, no matter what life had in store for us. And now, as if life had written its own perfect sequel, we had just found out we were expecting a little girl. The weight of that knowledge was both thrilling and overwhelming.

Pregnancy had never been easy on me, but this time, it was even harder. Between the relentless symptoms and the ever-present battle with lupus, my body felt like it was constantly at war with itself. Some days, I could barely move. Others, I could push through, willing myself to keep up with life as I knew it. But despite the exhaustion, the discomfort, and the endless doctor's appointments, there was something undeniably right about this. As if this was exactly where we were meant to be.

I closed my eyes, breathing in the cool evening air, thinking about the girl who had once stood in this very place—years ago, before the divorce, before the sickness, before Alex. That girl had been afraid, uncertain, holding on to things that no longer fit the person she was becoming. She had no idea what lay ahead. No idea that by stepping into the unknown, she would find everything she had ever needed.

Because in the end, it had never been just about the bookstore, or the divorce, or even the struggles that came with illness. It had always been about something deeper.

Love.

Family.

Purpose.

And it was in these things that I had learned to heal.

I turned and stepped back inside, letting the warmth of the store welcome me. The familiar scent of paper and ink wrapped around me, grounding me in the present. The soft rustle of turning pages and murmured conversations filled the air as the last few customers browsed the shelves. It still felt like home. It always had.

As I made my way to the back, my eyes landed on Alex, his frame bathed in the soft golden glow of the overhead lights. He was scanning the pages of a book, his brow furrowed in concentration. There was something about him in moments like this—so unguarded, so effortlessly a part of my world—that still made my heart swell.

He had become my partner in every sense of the word. In business. In love. In life. His presence had grounded me. His love had given me the courage to become the woman I had always wanted to be. "How's it looking?" I asked, leaning against a bookshelf, a small smile playing on my lips.

Alex looked up, his eyes softening the moment they met mine.

"It looks great," he said, closing the book and walking toward me. "I think this might be one of our best months yet."

His hand instinctively found my growing belly, his touch warm and reverent. Even after a year of marriage, I still wasn't used to how effortlessly he could make me feel safe.

I smiled, placing my hand over his. "I'm glad. It's been a lot of work, but I think it's finally paying off."

Alex tilted his head, his expression filled with something deeper than just pride. "Of course it is," he said, as if it was the most obvious thing in the world. "You've been working for this your whole life. I'm just happy I get to be a part of it."

His words settled into me, quiet and certain.

We had spent so many nights dreaming about this place, planning events, rearranging the layout, brainstorming ways to bring more life into the store. But it wasn't just about the business. It was about the life we had built together.

"I've been thinking," I said, taking a step closer. "About everything. About how far we've come."

He raised an eyebrow, his gaze steady. "What about it?"

"How much has changed," I whispered, emotion thick in my voice. "How much we've changed. I think… I think I'm finally where I'm supposed to be." Alex exhaled softly, his thumb brushing across my knuckles. "Me too, Elle," he murmured. "Me too."

For a moment, we just stood there, letting the weight of the moment settle between us. There was no need to rush forward. No need to plan for the next challenge. We had arrived. Together. The chime above the door rang, pulling us from our quiet bubble. Carter and Sam burst through the entrance, their laughter filling the space. It was the sound of life—of family.

Carter had grown taller, his voice beginning to carry the depth of his teenage years, but there was still a softness to him that made my heart ache with love. Sam, full of endless energy, bounded toward Alex without hesitation. Alex caught him effortlessly, lifting him into the air as Sam squealed with delight. Carter watched them, rolling his eyes with exaggerated exasperation, but the smile tugging at the corner of his mouth gave him away.

I stepped back, watching them, my heart swelling with something I couldn't quite put into words. This was my family.

It wasn't perfect. There were still hard days, still uncertainties that lingered in the background. But we had learned to work through them, to lean on each other when things felt unsteady.

The road to get here hadn't been easy. But it had been ours.

I walked toward the counter, running my fingers along the worn wood, feeling the heartbeat of the store beneath my palms. This place had seen my beginnings, my struggles, my transformation. It had held me in the hardest moments, and now, it held all the joy that had come after.

I glanced at Alex, then at the boys, and in that moment, I could see it so clearly—the full circle of it all.

The store was thriving.

The boys were growing.

And Alex and I were stronger than I had ever imagined we could be.

"How about we close up early tonight?" I said, glancing at Alex. "Take the boys out for dinner?"

Alex turned to me with a mischievous grin, his eyes full of love. "That sounds perfect. I think we've earned it."

And just like that, we were back in motion—our family, our future, moving forward together.

The life I had once thought impossible was unfolding before me, and it was more beautiful than I had ever dreamed.

As we walked out the door, the last rays of the sun slipping beneath the horizon, I couldn't help but smile.

It had taken everything to get here.

But the journey had been worth it.

This wasn't just the end of a story.

It was the beginning of another.

A life built not on perfection, but on resilience, love, and the unwavering belief that no matter where life takes us, we will always find our way home.

Because our story wasn't one out of a fairy tale.

But it was ours.

And that made it worth everything.

Acknowledgements

Writing this book has been a journey—one filled with passion, late nights, endless rewrites, and the unwavering support of those around me. There are so many people to thank, and while words will never fully capture my gratitude, I want to take a moment to acknowledge those who helped bring this story to life.

To my boys—my greatest inspiration. While the ages may not align exactly, the heart of Carter and Sam was drawn from the two most incredible young men in my life. Your laughter, resilience, and boundless energy have filled my world with so much love, and I hope this book serves as a reflection of the joy and chaos that comes with raising sons as remarkable as you. You are, and always will be, the best part of my life.

To my family and friends—thank you for listening to me talk about this book nonstop, for letting me bounce ideas off you, and for always encouraging me, even when I doubted myself. Your belief in me gave me the courage to keep writing, even on the hardest days.

To my editor—thank you for your patience, your keen eye, and your ability to take a first-time writer's words and help shape them into something stronger. I know it wasn't always easy, but your guidance has been invaluable, and I am beyond grateful for your time, dedication, and expertise.

And lastly, to the readers—whether you picked up this book on a whim, followed the journey from the beginning, or simply stumbled upon these pages, thank you. Thank you for taking a chance on this story, for allowing these characters to become a part of your world, and for proving that stories—whether fictional or real—have the power to connect us all.

This book is more than just words on a page. It is a piece of my heart, a labor of love, and a reminder that no matter where life takes us, we all have the power to rewrite our own stories.

With gratitude,

K.C